"Maybe you should think about staying in Spring Forest," Shane whispered, his tongue now in her belly button.

She froze, and she felt him freeze.

"Maybe I shouldn't have said that out loud." He moved back up so that they were at eye level, his hands gentle on her face. "Dammit."

"It's better you did," she said. "We should be careful with ourselves."

He looked directly into her eyes. "I want you, Bethany. I always have. This is my second chance, and second chances don't come along often. I'm not throwing it away. Is it a risk? Yeah, it is. But one worth taking."

Risk, risk, risk. She didn't put herself at risk anymore. It was how she lived her life. The *tenet* of her life.

She wished she could explain that this didn't feel real or possible. She could be here with him like this because Spring Forest was temporary; *he* was temporary. Meatball was temporary. She knew that and she never lost sight of it. Shane wasn't hers. Meatball wasn't hers. Wyatt certainly wasn't hers.

Dear Reader,

Back in 2014, I adopted a tiny black-and-white kitten, Cleo, with a cute black smudge on her white nose from a local animal shelter. In 2017, when I adopted a sweet, shy shepherd mix, Flash, from an all-breed rescue center, Cleo became his instant buddy, snuggling alongside his belly for naps, following him all over the house. These two furry creatures bring me so much joy. They're bundles of unconditional love and add so much to my life.

My love of animals makes me so happy to be part of this very special continuity series, Furever Yours. *Home is Where the Hound Is* kicks off our second visit to Spring Forest, North Carolina, and the Furever Paws Animal Rescue Center. Bethany Robeson, who used to have quite the reputation, returns to town after twelve long years and unexpectedly reunites with her old love, single father Shane Dupree. Suddenly, she's temporarily running Furever Paws, trying to find a home for a hard-to-place senior basset hound named Meatball—and trying *not* to fall for Shane (and his seven-month-old son) all over again.

I hope you enjoy Bethany, Shane and Meatball's story! I love to hear from readers, so please check out my website at melissasenate.com and feel free to friend me on Facebook and follow me on Twitter, where I post way too many pictures of my dog and cat!

Warmest regards,

Melissa Senate

Home is Where the Hound Is

MELISSA SENATE

HARLEQUIN
SPECIAL
EDITION

Special thanks and acknowledgment are given to Melissa Senate for her contribution to the Furever Yours miniseries.

HARLEQUIN®

SPECIAL EDITION™

Recycling programs
for this product may
not exist in your area.

ISBN-13: 978-1-335-40841-9

Home is Where the Hound Is

Copyright © 2022 by Harlequin Books S.A.

This edition published by arrangement with Harlequin Books S.A.

For questions and comments about the quality of this book, please contact us at CustomerService@Harlequin.com.

Harlequin Enterprises ULC
22 Adelaide St. West, 41st Floor
Toronto, Ontario M5H 4E3, Canada
www.Harlequin.com

Printed in U.S.A.

Melissa Senate has written many novels for
Harlequin and other publishers, including her debut,
See Jane Date, which was made into a TV movie. She
also wrote seven books for Harlequin Special Edition
under the pen name Meg Maxwell. Her novels have
been published in over twenty-five countries. Melissa
lives on the coast of Maine with her teenage son;
their rescue shepherd mix, Flash; and a lap cat named
Cleo. For more information, please visit her website,
melissasenate.com.

Books by Melissa Senate

Harlequin Special Edition

Dawson Family Ranch

For the Twins' Sake
Wyoming Special Delivery
A Family for a Week
The Long-Awaited Christmas Wish
Wyoming Cinderella
Wyoming Matchmaker
His Baby No Matter What

Furever Yours

Home is Where the Hound Is
A New Leash on Love

Visit the Author Profile page
at Harlequin.com for more titles.

Dedicated to the Midcoast Humane Society in Maine, and the Wags and Wiggles All-Breed Rescue in New Hampshire for the two bundles of furry love (my cat, Cleo, and my dog, Flash) who joined my family and bring us such joy.

Chapter One

Years ago, Bethany Robeson had figured out the secret cure for whatever ailed her. If she was feeling grumpy, had a bad day, got socked by old memories or had too many bills to pay, all she had to do was look for the nearest dog. And given that she'd worked in animal rescue until very recently, dogs had been aplenty. From purebreds to mixed breeds, from tiny toy poodles to shaggy medium-sized mutts to mighty Newfoundlands, a furry body and wagging tail would warm her heart and restore her spirit.

She needed that right now. She sat in her car in a parking spot on Main Street, windows down to let in the early spring breeze, and watched a beagle pad beside his owner on the sidewalk. The adorable dog stopped to sniff a patch of grass near the curb by the coffee shop, and Bethany grinned as he lifted his head and let out a joyful howl. *Ahoooo.*

The beagle was very helpful right now. Bethany had just arrived in Spring Forest, and being back here—for only the second time in twelve years— made her feel equally stabby and sad. And more than a little nervous about what she was about to face.

Questions. Rumors. Old classmates. *Particular* old classmates.

Bethany had been the black sheep of her hometown. Never mind that she'd been quiet, studious, had kept to herself and hadn't had her first kiss until her senior year. She'd been branded the town good-time girl in *middle school* because of who her mother was. Assumptions made, lies told, conclusions drawn.

As Bethany got out of her car, she wanted to jump back in and drive away. Which was silly. She *had* to be here to take care of some uncomfortable business. Then she'd leave. She'd be in Spring Forest a few days, tops. Besides, she and her supposed past were surely long forgotten in the small North Carolina town.

Or not.

Because the moment she shut the car door, she could hear whispers. About herself.

"Omigod, is that Bethany Robeson?"

"Did you hear she inherited Elliot Bradley's house?"

Audible gasp. "So he *was* her father?"

Bethany sighed. *You've got to be kidding me*, she thought as she walked over to the two women—yup, old classmates—sitting outside the coffee shop at a round table. "Number one," she said to them, "I can *hear* you. Number two, my life is none of your concern. Wasn't back in high school, isn't now."

Head held high, she pulled open the door to the coffee shop and walked in without waiting to listen to their stammered apologies or protests. The old Bethany, who hadn't known how to stand up for herself, was gone. She liked this new version of herself. A little time, some life experience and many years spent far from Spring Forest had taken care of that. She ordered an iced mocha and glanced out the front window. The two women who'd been talking about her were getting up, taking turns staring at her as they left. Some things never changed. But Bethany *had*.

Thing was, though, Bethany also wanted to know if she was Elliot Bradley's daughter. Her mother had been his longtime mistress, and despite their discretion, everyone in town had seemed to know about the affair. Elliot had never come to the apartment be-

fore Bethany was asleep, had never spent the night,
yet she'd spied them together several times. One in-
stance stood out. She'd been twelve, had woken up
in the middle of the night and had seen them by the
door of her and her mother's apartment, whispering
goodbye with such feeling in their eyes and voices,
and then kissing—the way couples did in the movies.
Her relationship with her mother had always been
complicated, but in that moment, she'd known one
thing with absolute certainty. Her mother loved Elliot. And he loved her.

That love didn't change anything, of course. They
were cheating, running around behind Elliot's wife's
back—for years. Decades. At the very least, for all of
Bethany's life, until her mother's death. But something about the *depth* of their feelings for each other
had affected Bethany, both positively and negatively.

People were complicated. Life was complicated.
Love was complicated.

Vows shouldn't be, though. Maybe that was why
Bethany had never gotten married. Lack of trust in
the institution. Or maybe that was just an excuse.
She'd really tried to figure it out over the years. She'd
gotten her heart broken hard at eighteen, not even
by the guy involved—talk about *complicated*—and
that had made her wary of even committing to relationships.

She'd surprised herself by her trust in Shane Dupree back then. At seventeen, she'd had years of practice in expecting disdain from others. She was twelve when she first heard the word *trashy* thrown at her, fifteen when *slut* had been written in marker on her high school locker, on her desk. She'd spent most of high school running into bathroom stalls to quietly break down and cry only to find cruel things written about her on the walls. *Bethany Robeson is such a whore. Like mother like daughter.*

She'd gotten through those years by studying hard, working part-time, volunteering and keeping very busy. If she developed a crush on a boy she'd tamp down her feelings, afraid he'd shun her the way girls did, afraid he'd expect the rumors to be true. She turned down every boy who asked her out. The ones who didn't like that just acted as if she'd said yes and then spread rumors about what they'd done during their "date." That was how she'd ended up seventeen and unkissed—with a very bad reputation.

Then came senior year, when everything changed—including her unexpected friendship with Shane Dupree. Her relationship with the very cute guy who sat beside her in history class had turned into everything Bethany had ever dreamed of. He'd been her first *everything*.

Don't think about him, she told herself as she

sipped her iced mocha on the way out of the coffee shop. *Focus on the house Elliot Bradley left you and getting rid of it.*

Was he her father? The rumors had trailed Bethany all her life and now, at age thirty, she still wasn't sure. The inheritance sure made it seem so. They'd really only known each other in passing. He'd said maybe ten words to her over the decades, a hello here and there around town if it couldn't be avoided.

He hadn't come to her mom's funeral. That had made her certain he wasn't her father.

Maybe there'd been no one else to leave the house to but the daughter of his mistress of twenty-five years. He had no family. His wife had passed four years ago—a year after Bethany's mother—and there were no children. Except perhaps her. Her mom hadn't been one to give straight answers, not when Bethany was a child and had asked repeatedly, and not even on the day she died. Maybe her mother truly hadn't known either. Local talk made it clear that before she'd met Elliot, Kate Robeson had had a few other boyfriends, then the sun rose and set on the tall, handsome lawyer. Bethany had come along within a year of Kate meeting Elliot. She was either his child—or one of the previous boyfriends'. The question had frustrated her over the years to the point that she'd made a deal with herself to stop thinking about it for her own peace of mind.

But then Elliot, whose sterling reputation hadn't been the least tarnished by his extramarital affair in a typical double standard, had brought it all back up again by leaving Bethany his beautiful colonial on Oak Street.

Right next door to the Dupree family.

Another…issue.

Chances were pretty good that the Duprees still lived there. The house had been in the family for three generations. After she fortified herself with enough caffeine, Bethany would drive over to Elliot's place. If she were lucky, and sometimes she was, she wouldn't run into a Dupree while she was pulling into the driveway next door, intending to give the house a quick once-over to see how fast she could sell it.

Her plan: get it on the market ASAP and then put Spring Forest in her rearview mirror.

Iced coffee finished, she tossed the cup in a trash can and headed to her car, almost colliding with a woman walking a basset hound with an Adopt Me banner over his back. Bethany glanced at the woman's sweatshirt logo: Furever Paws Animal Rescue. A place Bethany knew well. The dog, low to the ground with soulful brown eyes and long droopy ears, was so beautiful.

Bethany asked if she could pet him, getting a smile and a "Go right ahead" and "Are you interested in adopting Meatball? He's been with Furever Paws for too long and needs a loving home."

Meatball. Aww. Bethany knelt beside him, her heart unexpectedly clenching, the dog's soft hair feeling so good in her hands as he sheepishly looked at her, head cast down.

Or maybe not so unexpectedly. Yes, dogs always cheered her up, but she was quick to empathize with them, too—especially when they seemed to be having their own rough time. Meatball was overweight, definitely on the shy side and appeared to be in his senior years. Advanced age alone would make it a struggle to find him a forever home. Add the weight and timidity, and a darling dog was left behind. Bethany was practically an expert in hard-to-adopt dogs. Until just two weeks ago, she'd been the assistant director of an animal shelter three hours south of Spring Forest, but the place had closed due to lack of funds. Bethany had practically gone bankrupt trying to save the shelter. She'd exhausted herself, working so many extra hours to fundraise and then, when it was hopeless, to help place their dear animals with fosters or other area shelters.

If only the call from Elliot's lawyer about the house had come two weeks earlier, she could have single-handedly saved the shelter. But it was too late, the building sold and already razed for a big-box store as if the staff and volunteers hadn't left huge pieces of their hearts there.

She gave Meatball a good rub, earning a slight raise of his sweet face. Aww. "I'm just visiting," she said to the woman, noting the pin under the Furever Paws logo: *Volunteer.* Just as Bethany had been for years before she'd left town.

A couple with an excited young child came up to the woman and Meatball, asking questions, so Bethany smiled and hurried to her car.

How can anyone resist you, Meatball? she wondered, turning on the engine. *What a sweet, calm dog.*

Thinking of the needs of animals like Meatball just reinforced her plan for her future. She'd sell Elliot Bradley's house and use the money to open her own shelter back in Berryville, where she lived. That was part two of the plan. Hard to adopt dogs—bring 'em.

She wanted nothing to do with Elliot Bradley's money for herself. But funding for a nonprofit animal rescue that would find loving homes for dogs and cats and the occasional rabbit or bird or lizard or rodent? You bet she'd use every penny of the money for the good in that.

On the way to Elliot's house—she still couldn't think of it as *her* house—she tried to steel herself.

She slowly drove past the Dupree home just as the white front door opened. Her heart sped up and she quickly pulled into Elliot's driveway, slinking down and turning away.

Ugh. Please don't let it be Shane's mother about to come outside. The woman who drove me out of town twelve years ago just when I'd finally found a reason to stay.

Bethany dared a peek at the neighboring home's front door.

It wasn't Anna Dupree.

No. The person walking out of the house, holding the pink leash of a cinnamon-colored Chihuahua, was at least six foot two. Tall and leanly muscular. With slightly long, sexy sandy-brown hair.

And had a blue-and-white baby carrier strapped to his chest, a big-cheeked baby surveying Oak Street.

Bethany's heart was now pounding.

Shane Dupree was a father?

That shouldn't surprise her. He was thirty, just like her. And hadn't he always wanted a big family?

She ducked farther down in her seat, but she was unable to look away.

Shane was now locking the door.

Her heart beating way too fast, she sat in the car, looking to the left, away from the Dupree house. Maybe he wouldn't see her.

"Ruff, ruff-ruff! Ruff! Grrr-ruff!"

Bethany glanced over to see the Chihuahua dashing to her car, barking bloody murder.

Oh boy.

"Princess Dupree!" called a familiar voice.

Bethany couldn't help but smile at that. Not only did Shane Dupree have a Chihuahua, but she was named Princess.

Maybe the wife had named the dog.

"Grrr-woof! Grrr-ruff!" The dog barked and barked.

"So she gets the full name treatment when she's naughty, huh?" Bethany said, leaning toward the passenger-side window as Shane got closer. Where she got the nerve to actually speak, the light lilt of humor in her voice, was beyond her.

He stopped dead in his tracks.

He stared at her. Hard.

"Bethany?"

Dammit, those blue eyes of his. Those eyes had looked into hers for six months twelve years ago and made her feel hopeful. Six months that had actually changed her entire life, how she felt about herself and people and possibilities.

And then it was all over, and she'd never seen those eyes again.

Until now.

She sucked in a deep breath and got out of the car,

staying on the driver's side. She needed the width of her SUV between them. "Yup, it's me," she said over the roof of the vehicle.

He was still staring, then seemed to remember the loose dog and knelt down to reattach the collar, holding the leash tightly. "She slipped her collar," he added, standing up. "My mother insists on keeping it too loose."

Please don't let Anna come outside. She was not ready to deal with *her* too. "So this is your mother's dog?"

Talking about the Chihuahua was easier than asking about the baby. Name, age, how long Shane had been married.

Except her gaze slipped to his hand and there was no ring.

Shane nodded. "I'm taking care of Princess until my mom returns from a spa vacation with her sister. Today's day one of five. I'm already wondering if I'll survive, and I'm a dog trainer by profession." He smiled, the smile that used to transfix her, and shook his head.

She barely registered her relief that she wouldn't have to deal with his mom while in town because she was so focused on the last thing he said. "A dog trainer? You didn't become a doctor?"

"Nope," he said. And didn't elaborate. She wondered what happened. He'd been so focused on his goal of becoming a physician. His dream had been to become a rural doctor, to help those who lived very far from town and the nearest hospital.

For a moment, they just looked at each other. She could hardly believe she was standing just feet away from Shane, talking to him. After all these years.

He came around the side of the SUV, and the full view of him, this man she'd fallen so hard for back then, almost made her knees buckle.

"And this little guy," he said, glancing down at the baby on his chest, "is Wyatt. Seven months and teething. Wyatt, meet Bethany Robeson. An old friend of Daddy's."

"He's adorable," she said, smiling at the sweet-faced baby, one tooth in his gummy mouth. He looked a lot like Shane.

"I remember you wanted five kids," she said. "What number is this cutie?" Again, how she sounded so casual, like she ran into Shane Dupree all the time, was beyond her.

"One and only," he said. "I was married…it didn't work out."

"Sorry," she said. And she was. She'd never been married herself, but she knew what heartache felt like. And the dissolution of a marriage had to be really rough stuff. Still, she was grateful she wouldn't be bumping into him and his wife—that would have been too painful.

He looked away for a moment, giving Wyatt's brown hair a gentle caress, then turned back to her. "I did hear that Elliot left you the house. I hate gossip, and I know you do, too. Or used to. But the subject's come up."

Bethany had no doubt the entire town knew. She stared over at the gorgeous white colonial with the red door and black shutters. A classic. The couple of times when she'd gone to Shane's after they'd become friends, and then more, she'd glance at the Bradley house and wonder how such an awful person—a cheating liar—could live in such a pretty home.

"Before I drove to Spring Forest, I arranged to have the power turned on in my name. I thought I'd just go in and look around, see what needs doing before I can get it on the market," she said, "but now the thought of going inside makes me feel sick."

"Yeah, I can imagine." He cleared his throat. "If you need some backup going in, Princess, Wyatt and I are available."

"Grrr-ruff!"

Bethany smiled at the tiny light brown dog. "Is that agreement, Princess?"

Princess stared her down. No wagging tail. She

gave a little growl and looked like she wanted to bite Bethany's leg.

Eh, Bethany would win her over. That was her job. Or had been. Either way, she had plenty of experience winning over the scared or the simply untrained— and she'd say Princess Dupree was simply untrained.

"I've got five days to get this dog in shape," Shane said. "And by in shape, I mean well-behaved. All on the down low. My mother says Princess listens to her *enough* and doesn't want me 'being mean' to her, so she's never let me work with her. I've tried to explain the rudiments of dog training till I'm blue in the face, but…"

Bethany smiled and nodded. "I know all about that. I've been working in animal rescue for years."

"Seems we both got rerouted from our original plans," he said.

My original plan was to get the hell out of Spring Forest. But then I met you and couldn't imagine leaving. Until…

Old news. That she didn't want to think about anymore.

"Come on," he said. "I'll walk you in."

She bit her lip and took another glance at the house. She definitely didn't want to go in there by herself. She hadn't realized until this moment just how spooked the house would make her.

With her mind churning over memories of how she and her mother had been treated in town, she just wanted to stick a For Sale sign in the yard and get out of here.

But Shane had always had a way of making her feel stronger. More sure of herself.

"Thank you," she said. "And thank *you*, Princess," she added to the Chihuahua. "You might be little, but I can already tell you're tough. And I need tough surrounding me to walk in there."

Princess eyed her. No sweet head tilt, but no growl either. Hey, it was a start.

Bethany got out the silver key the lawyer had sent her and headed up the walkway, Shane, Wyatt and Princess right behind her. She could smell Shane's soap or shampoo, something clean and citrusy. She could feel his presence, all that height, his long, lean body in faded jeans and a brown leather jacket.

Twelve years. And here he was, inches from her.

And she had thought dealing with the *house* would test her?

Bethany Robeson. Back in town. Twelve years had done little to dim his reaction to her.

He followed her inside the house, catching the scent of a light floral perfume. Shane had always found Bethany beautiful, but she was even more so now. She was tall, five-seven or -eight, with silky long brown hair shot through with honeyed strands, a bit longer now than it had been the last time he'd seen her, and green eyes that had always been impossible to look away from. She was strong and curvy and so damned sexy in jeans and a sweater that he couldn't drag his gaze off her.

Their brief romance senior year of high school had been intense. A slow start and then *fire*. Given her reputation, what was whispered about her, he'd felt wrong for fantasizing about Bethany when they'd just been getting to know each other, as if he were adding to it all, but he couldn't help it. Besides, nothing about the rumors matched the girl he'd known. It had taken Shane two weeks to even get close enough to *kiss* her. And the look in her eyes when he had… she'd been so beautifully surprised and delighted. How could anyone have taken a single look at her and not seen how sweet and amazing she was?

All these years, he'd never forgotten her, barely stopped thinking about her.

The girl who'd gotten away. Maybe that was it.

More like the girl who'd dumped him with a five-second phone call, leaving him unable to understand what the hell had happened.

Good riddance, his mother had said when he told

her that Bethany had left town, just like that. *To bad rubbish*, she had added under her breath.

But he'd heard it. Loud and clear. Shane, eighteen then, newly graduated from high school, had stopped speaking to his mother after that until she actually apologized for what she'd said, something Anna Dupree rarely did. He'd forgiven her then, but he'd never forgotten it and though he never stopped loving his mother, her meanness, over someone special to him, had done its damage. He'd distanced himself in countless ways. Things were rough in their household in those days, compounded by his father's troubles, and the way that Shane's plans, dreams he'd had for years, disintegrated.

All water under the ole bridge.

What mattered now was Wyatt. Everything he did, he did for that little human who he loved so much that sometimes it stole his breath. He had his son, he had his business, Barkyard Boarding—and those were the most important things in the world to him. Sure, he was glad that his business was doing well. In fact, it was one of the most successful dog boarding and training facilities in the county. The money it brought in allowed him to afford the ridiculously large four-bedroom house his now ex-wife had wanted in the fancy Kingdom Creek development. But he didn't need the house or all that money he'd earned.

Nope, his son and his work. Those were his true priorities. Everything else, he'd learned to take as it came. When his marriage couldn't hold together, he wished Nina well and was pleased to have a low-drama divorce and an amicable shared custody arrangement. She had a serious boyfriend now, a nice, dependable accountant who played peekaboo with Wyatt every time he dropped off Wyatt at their even bigger house. Shane was happy for them. He didn't bear grudges and he didn't dwell on the past.

But now, here was Bethany. A piece of his past walking back into his life and rattling him more than anything had in a long time.

No, thanks. He didn't need the roller coaster. Not with a baby to single parent half the week and every other weekend.

"Huh," Bethany said, looking around. "The place is a bit more run-down than I expected. And I can't see getting a decent price with that outdated kitchen. I'll have to put some work in."

A lot of work. The door to the dining room was hanging off one hinge. And Elliot's cigar habit had yellowed the walls.

After a trip upstairs revealed the bathroom was in even more dire need of updating than the kitchen,

Shane could already tell it would be a couple of weeks at least before the house would be ready for a For Sale sign.

Bethany sighed, her gaze on the cracked pink sink, then moving over to the pink bathtub, the grout in need of replacing. "I don't have money to invest in repairs." She shook her head and frowned. "I guess I'll just have to list it as is."

"Or," Shane said, "you could talk to Harris Vega. He flips houses. Sometimes, if you don't have much to spend upfront, he'll take a percentage of the sale in exchange for the price for materials and labor. You'd be amazed at what he can do on a limited budget too." He reached into his wallet and searched the many business cards stuffed in the little compartments. "Here."

She took the card and read it. "Um, thanks. I'll call him for sure."

They headed back downstairs. "And I'll help you," Shane said before he even thought about it, noting the bits of tape covering holes in the window screen. "I can take care of the small stuff—get that closet door rehung correctly, clear out some of the heavy furniture. I don't think those massive, beat-up leather his-and-her recliners in the living room will be a draw."

Bethany stared at the recliners, then looked at

him. "You don't have to do that. Between Wyatt and your business, I'm sure your days are pretty packed."

"I'll be coming round to Mom's place to take care of Princess four times a day. So I'll be right here any-way." *And I want to help you.* Something about her had always brought out the white knight in him that wanted to support and protect her. It was kind of in-convenient that that instinct hadn't gone away after she'd stepped on his heart…but he couldn't see that sad, overwhelmed, all-too-familiar look on her face without wanting to make it better. No matter what had happened between them, she'd been very spe-cial to him once. "And that way, you won't have to be alone here, going through the clutter. And man, is there clutter," he added, glancing around.

"I see you haven't changed," she said. "Still re-ally nice."

"Oh, trust me. I've changed in a lot of ways. But I know being here has to be hard for you. In town *and* in this house. So, I'm helping. And that's final."

She smiled. "I really appreciate that. Thank you," she said slowly, as if forcing herself to accept his offer. He could tell she was uncomfortable. As was he. "I wasn't planning on staying here, but since I won't be able to wrap this up quickly, the way I'd hoped, I can't justify spending money on a motel or anything. I just have to remember that it's only a house. It's not going to bite me. It's not haunted."

"It's definitely just a house," he said.

Except houses were never just houses. They were pieces of history. Filled with memories. He and Bethany had spent a lot of time in the Robesons' rental apartment above the bar where her mother had worked. The place had been small and shabby and often smelled like the onion rings constantly cooking downstairs, but all he'd cared about was that he was with Bethany. The apartment had become special to both of them.

"I am surprised at how run-down the house is," she said. "Elliot was a wealthy lawyer."

"Yeah, he definitely let things slide. Once he was on his own, he kept to himself more, stopped accepting invitations."

"The guilt got him, I suppose," she said. "Though it hadn't seemed to while he was carrying on the affair."

"Maybe the loneliness, then."

She wrapped her arms around herself and turned away. "Well," she said.

He waited for her to add to that, but she didn't.

Her shoulders sagged, and he wanted to go over and hold her. But he'd smush Wyatt. And possibly his own heart as well, but he was better at protecting his son than at protecting himself. Especially when the urge to comfort Bethany was so strong.

But he wasn't going anywhere near a romantic reunion. He was done with romance. At least for now, while Wyatt was a baby. While he had so much to juggle. He'd failed at love enough to not dust himself off and get back up again. This time, he was staying down.

Especially because it was clear Bethany would be sticking around for a few weeks to get the house ready for sale.

Long enough for him to fall for her all over again. And he couldn't let that happen.

It's you and me, Wyatt, he said silently to his son with a gentle caress on his brown hair.

"Ba!" Wyatt said with his gummy smile.

"Is that so?" Bethany asked, laughing, coming over and bending down a bit to Wyatt's level.

She reached out and touched his son's cheek, the sweet gesture going straight to his heart.

Yeah, he was in trouble here.

Chapter Two

As Bethany closed the door behind Shane and his adorable son, she practically sagged against the paint-chipped wood. This was all too much. The house. Shane. Discovering that Shane was divorced with a baby and here in town.

And going to be next door four times a day.

She dropped down on the leather sofa, but realized she was staring at the his-and-her recliners and bolted up and moved over to the windows. She didn't want to think about Elliot Bradley and his wife sitting in their matching chairs, having a glass of wine or cup of tea, watching TV at the end of the day. Being in this house filled her with questions. Questions she wasn't sure she wanted the answers to.

She had to get out of here. If Shane hadn't very unexpectedly been leaving his mother's house when she'd arrived, if he hadn't gallantly offered to come in with her, she probably would have raced out after a minute. Unsettled. Alone.

I'll be back tonight around seven to take care of Princess, he'd said as she'd walked him to the door not five minutes ago. *How about I stop over once I'm done, and I'll make a list of what I can take care of?*

She'd almost told him she'd be fine here on her own, no need for him to help.

But she *wouldn't* be fine. The house overwhelmed her in every regard. And besides, she wasn't handy with power tools. Then there was the uncomfortable truth that she wanted to see Shane again.

After one brief interaction, all those memories she'd tamped down the past twelve years had come raging back. His kindness, their connection, their red-hot chemistry, the way he'd made her feel—that anything was possible, after all. He'd been adorable back then, tall and lanky and so cute she could stare at his face for hours. Now, he was very much a man.

And a father. When Bethany had looked at Wyatt, snuggled safely against Shane's chest, she'd felt such a stirring. *Because Shane Dupree was your first love, cut short, and you're afflicted by a bad case of might-have-been.* On the drive to Spring Forest, she'd wondered what she'd find out about Shane—that he was married with three kids. That of course he'd moved on. But she'd never expected to find him single... with a baby. He didn't seem quite available, though, which was a good thing. She couldn't go there. Not with Shane.

At the door he'd asked if she'd be okay here by herself, and she had the urge to wrap him in a hug. To thank him for caring when there was no one in her life anymore to care. She might have had issues with how Kate Robeson had lived her life, but her mom had either called or texted every single night at 10:00 p.m. How's my girl?

She grabbed her purse from the coffee table, her eyes welling as she hurried to the door. She locked up and practically ran to her car. Sometimes she missed her mother so fiercely. Especially now, when she felt particularly alone. Untethered.

She knew what she needed right now. Furever Paws. She needed shelter owners Birdie and Bunny Whitaker's warmth and wisdom. And she needed the animals. Surely there would be dogs that needed walking, cats that needed playing with, litter boxes that needed changing.

Furever Paws had just about rescued Bethany

back in middle school when she'd first started volunteering. The place, the work, the dear sisters who'd started the rescue center—everything about the place had been just as much a refuge for her as it had been for the many dogs and cats needing help finding forever homes. Bethany had volunteered there until the day she'd left town.

The drive over to Little Creek Road took barely five minutes. She pulled into the gravel parking lot, taking in the one-story structure that was now painted a sunny yellow rather than the gray she remembered even just five years ago. The rescue center had been rebuilt and expanded after it was wrecked in a storm, but the Furever Paws logo, a cat and dog silhouette inside a heart painted on the front of the building, was the same. She smiled at it. How many hours had she spent here as a teen, forgetting everything once she walked inside?

A young man with a volunteer pin sat at the front desk, typing away at a desktop computer. Bethany glanced around, feeling herself calm immediately. Animal rescue centers always felt like home, and this place in particular had been her sanctuary during some really rough times. Seeing it looking so well-kept and freshly done up was like seeing an old friend looking better than ever. Not everything was exactly as she remembered it, but she liked all the changes that she could see. The walls, now painted a soothing pale blue, were lined with paintings of dogs and cats for sale by local artists. Bethany's heart skipped a beat when she saw one of Meatball, the basset hound she'd met on Main Street earlier. She just might buy that painting. She'd hang it in her condo when she got back to Berryville.

The volunteer at the desk looked up and smiled and welcomed her to the Furever Paws Animal Rescue. Bethany asked if Birdie or Bunny was around, and the guy tapped at an intercom.

A few moments later, Birdie Whitaker came out of the door behind the lobby. When she saw Bethany, she grinned. Birdie was in her midsixties now, but she seemed hardly changed at all by the passing years since Bethany had last seen her. She was still tall and strong with short graying brown hair. And her fashion sense clearly hadn't changed, since she was wearing a Furever Paws sweatshirt embroidered with black cats. Hard to adopt. Easy to love.

"Bethany! So good to see you! It's been a long time." Birdie swept her into a hug. Interesting. Birdie Whitaker was one of the kindest people Bethany had ever known—same as her sister, Bunny. But the Birdie she remembered was not the demonstrative type. Big hugs were not her style. Not that Bethany had any complaints. Boy, did she need one right now.

She squeezed Birdie back, and decided to answer the unasked question of what she was doing in town this long after she'd left it behind.

"I'm sure you heard the news, that I inherited El-liot Bradley's house?"

Birdie grimaced. "I hate gossip, but I did hear. Is that why you're back in Spring Forest?"

Bethany nodded.

"And how long do you think you'll be around?" Birdie asked.

"The house needs some work so it'll be a couple weeks, maybe three till I can list it for sale." She bit her lip, feeling the pull to find an animal and give it some attention. "Hey, we shouldn't just be standing around. Put me to work while we catch up. I know there's always tons to do at an animal rescue."

"Got that right," Birdie said. "I was about to make my rounds on the dogs, see how everyone's doing."

Bethany could use a lot of dog love right now. As they headed down the hallway, offices on the left and the dog kennels and cat room to the right, Bethany could hear some barking. Shelter dogs were always excited when someone was coming—whether for a meal, a walk, or some playtime. People interested in adopting sometimes dropped by to take a look at the dogs on-site, but the pooches at Furever Paws were primarily here because they weren't adoption-ready or hadn't yet been matched with a foster home.

"How is it being back?" Birdie asked as they passed the large viewing window at the cat room. Kennels of all sizes with soft blankets inside lined the space, and the kitty condos had several cats lounging, surveying the room as they groomed their faces with their paws. An open area at the back led to a small screened-in porch where the cats could watch the backyard birds all they wanted. "Has it been five years?"

Bethany nodded. "I wish I'd been here when the shelter got hit by the tornado. I would have loved to lend a hand in the rebuilding efforts." Two years ago, Furever Paws had almost been completely lost— twice over. First, the storm had done terrible damage. Then, when it came time to file an insurance claim, they'd run into a deeper problem. Turned out that one of Birdie and Bunny's brothers had long ago embezzled *a lot* of money from the shelter and they'd been shocked to discover their insurance had been allowed to lapse, leaving them with no funds to rebuild. But their nephew, Grant Whitaker, had made a smart business deal involving their land, and between that and the community pitching in on the cleanup and rebuilding, the rescue had come back bigger and better.

Bethany had actually been dealing with a storm crisis of her own during that time; it was the beginning of the end for the shelter where she'd been assistant director. She'd spoken to both Birdie and Bunny back then, and the sisters had known she would have been there to help them if she could. Then another storm had done further damage and there was just no coming back from it.

"I'm just sorry your rescue didn't make it," Birdie said, tilting her head to the left, then the right and staring at Bethany as if she had an idea. "Okay, now this is going to make me sound very opportunistic, but I have to ask."

"Ask what?"

Birdie took both her hands. "Would you consider taking on the role of temporary director of Furever Paws? Our current director, my niece-in-law Rebekah Whitaker, has been the director for the past two years but she had to scale back on her hours since the birth of her twins. Richard and I have been keeping things going with the help of even more volunteers than usual, but the shelter isn't operating as smoothly as it should."

"Richard?" Bethany repeated, even as Birdie's offer echoed in her head. Becoming director, temporary or not, would mean committing to Spring Forest until either Rebekah came back full time or Birdie found someone else. That was different from sticking around for "a couple of weeks" to see a house readied for market.

But how on earth could Bethany ever turn down Birdie Whitaker? Besides, having a wonderful reason to be in Spring Forest—and an excuse to spend most of her days with the animals she loved—would make everything to do with Elliot's house easier to bear.

"Yes, Richard," Birdie said, a smile widening on her face. "Oh—I mean Doc J."

Doc J, Richard Jackson, had been the shelter's veterinarian for as long as Bethany could remember. But she'd never, ever heard Birdie refer to him as *Richard*. In fact, had she ever seen that particular smile on Birdie's face? She looked like a woman in love.

Bethany grinned and narrowed her eyes. "I've clearly missed *a lot*."

Birdie squeezed her hand, and they headed a bit farther down the hall to look into the dog kennel room. "Well, Richard and I have been a thing for a while now. In fact, we live together in the farmhouse!"

Bethany gasped and pulled Birdie into a hug. "That's great! I'm so happy for you! I remember Richard—Doc J—as a wonderful man and such a compassionate veterinarian. And what about Bunny?"

"Oh, my sister is off on her own adventure in love. Bunny's been traveling around the country in an RV with her beau, a man named Stew Redmond who she'd been conversing with online for years. I don't know when she'll come home or if she will at all. She calls often and sounds very happy."

Wow! "I'm so thrilled for the two of you," Bethany said.

"And what about you?" Birdie asked. "Have you found your guy?"

Why did Shane Dupree flit into her mind?

"No success there. I've had a few relationships but nothing has worked out. Not that I expected them to. I've always been a loner."

Birdie patted her hand. "I said the same for years. Turns out you have to be open to it. Love, I mean. It's not easy when you've been guarded your whole life."

Tell me about it.

Bethany couldn't help her frown. "I'd been in town all of five minutes when I heard two women, old classmates, start gossiping about me. 'Is she El-liot Bradley's daughter? Is that why he left her the house?'" She grimaced and shook her head.

"Eh, ignore those busybodies. You're the best,

Bethany Robeson. And I'm a tough judge of character."

Bethany grinned. Birdie sure was. Part of her wanted to ask Birdie if she thought Elliot was her father, and if that was why he'd left her the house. But Birdie wasn't one to speculate. *No sense in yammering about what's what until you* know *what's what*, she'd always said.

"I mean, would I have offered you the job of temporary director of Furever Paws otherwise?" Birdie asked.

"I'm happy to help," Bethany said, sticking out her hand.

"Oh, I'm a hugger now," Birdie said, wrapping her in another warm embrace. "Come on," she said, slinging an arm around Bethany's shoulders. "I'll give you a brief rundown on the dogs and cats and other animals that are here, then introduce you to the staff. We have a great group. Then maybe you can start in earnest tomorrow morning?" she added with a hopeful smile.

"You got it," Bethany said.

The relief on her dear old friend's face was evident. As Birdie opened the door to the dog room, barking greeted them, but the noise settled down as they passed by the kennels. Just a handful of currently housed dogs. Birdie gave her the promised rundown as they walked, but suddenly Bethany stopped, hand to her heart.

"Meatball!" she exclaimed, peering in the kennel at the adorable basset hound curled up in a big soft bed, a squishy toy bone beside his chin, which rested on the rim of the bed.

"Know this sweet boy?" Birdie asked.

Bethany smiled at Meatball. "I happened to meet him today in town. What a darling. Look at that face, those eyes, those droopy ears!"

Birdie nodded. "I know, but I've had a heck of a time finding a foster placement for him, let alone a forever home. Between being a very shy senior citizen and a good fifteen pounds overweight, it makes him tricky to place. Getting him to a healthy weight will require committing to a gentle regimen, and without a full-time director, everyone's had to take on extra roles and Meatball hasn't really gotten the attention he needs."

"Aww," Bethany said. "I'd foster him but the house will be undergoing work so maybe I can just 'foster' him here. I'll work with him while I'm director. I'm already smitten."

"Great," Birdie said. She bent down toward the sweet basset hound. "Hear that, Meatball? You're about to get a big dose of Bethany love."

Bethany grinned and put her fingers in the kennel, earning a sniff and a tail wag from the dog.

Two volunteers came through the door to walk the two puppies under veterinary care, and so Bethany bid Meatball goodbye to meet the young women. Within a half hour, she'd met everyone in the shelter and got the new lay of the land. Directing an animal rescue meant responsibility for everything—taking in new strays and owner surrenders, arranging for veterinary care, assessing readiness for adoption, finding foster homes, fundraising, managing the budget, training staff and volunteers, and lots of petting. But of course, the perks of a lick on the cheek, a wagging tail made the very hard job of animal rescue worth every moment.

Just as Bethany was about to head to the empty office to make it her own, the front door opened and in padded a skinny, dirty mixed breed dog, some kind of short-haired shepherd, on a leash that was held by none other than Shane Dupree.

"Nice to see you, Shane," Birdie said. She turned to Bethany. "I know you're not officially starting till tomorrow, but I've got some work to catch up on. Mind handling this?"

Bethany caught the hint of smile in Birdie's tone as the woman didn't wait for an answer before she headed out of the lobby. Bethany had told Birdie everything on her way out of town twelve years ago, and the woman probably thought she was helping by giving them a chance to talk. Little did Birdie know, her matchmaking wouldn't go anywhere. There wasn't going to be a romantic reunion. There was no reason to think that Shane wanted one—and for her part, Bethany definitely didn't.

She didn't belong in Spring Forest. Once she'd taken care of why she was here, once Rebekah came back full time or Birdie found a permanent director for Furever Paws, Bethany would get in her car and leave.

She'd been a humiliated, crushed mess when she'd left town twelve years ago. It had taken her a solid year to stop tearing up about Shane every other minute. Everything about Spring Forest, with the exception of Furever Paws, meant heartache for Bethany.

And now, Shane Dupree, standing right there looking so good, the sight of him reminding her of a time when she foolishly believed in happily-ever-after, was a package deal. Not just one Dupree to love and lose, but *two*.

Chapter Three

"We seem to be in the same place at the same time a lot today," Shane said, keeping a tight hold on the leash.

Bethany knelt down beside the dog and reached out the back of her hand slowly to position it under the black nose. The dog shyly inched up to give her a sniff, and when Bethany gave his throat a few scratches and said, "Good boy," he practically melted against her. "Aww, he seems scared but definitely sweet and gentle. Where'd you find him?"

Shane knelt down too and gave the dog a pat. "Someone let him loose on my property at Barkyard Boarding. Dogs are all too often abandoned there. Why people just don't bring them here, I don't know."

"Oh, they do. When I volunteered here, dogs were always being turned out of cars at the edge of the property. A few times I stayed overnight to watch over dogs or cats recovering from surgeries and I'd hear a car door open, a car peel away, and then barking. I'd open the front door, and there would be a confused new stray." She shook her head. "This guy is certainly very cute."

"I need to talk to someone about Furever Paws taking him in," he said.

"You already are. Meet the shelter's new temporary director."

"A house and a job all in one afternoon?" He smiled. "Welcome to Spring Forest, Bethany Robeson." It felt so natural to talk to her like this. This was Bethany, his Bethany. The connection between them, which she'd severed long ago, had plugged right back in, their chemistry, on all levels, just as strong as ever. And that could be a problem. Bethany wasn't going to be an acquaintance unless he worked very hard at it.

He would. He'd been through some hard times the past year, his life uprooted. As long as he kept reminding himself that he and Wyatt didn't need any more upheaval, surely he could keep things purely… friendly between him and Bethany.

Whenever he felt himself weakening, he'd just mentally replay the way she'd dumped him with that cold five-second phone call the day after graduation—and drove out of town, never looking back. She'd smashed his heart, changed him—irrevocably.

"Oh, trust me on the word *temporary*," she said. "By the time the house is ready to list and then sells, either Rebekah will be ready to resume her job full-time or Birdie will find a permanent director."

Shane knew Rebekah and her husband. They had their hands full with their six-month-old twins, who'd been in the NICU the first couple of months. Because Shane's son was just a month older, Shane had gotten close with the couple, particularly Grant, nephew of the owners of Furever Paws. Shane knew that Rebekah felt guilty for only being able to work very part-time at the rescue and wasn't sure when—if—she'd be back full time.

"And as for this sweet guy," she said, giving the stray one last pat and standing up, "Furever Paws policy has always been to take in all animals with nowhere to go. If we don't have room, we'll find room. But it shouldn't be a problem. I saw quite a few empty kennels in the dog room. I'll take this guy over to Doc J's clinic and get him checked out to make sure he doesn't need to be quarantined. The doctor's retired from his own practice but volunteers his services full time here." She'd gotten the full update from Birdie while getting the tour.

"I'll go with you," Shane said, surprising himself. "I feel kind of responsible for this guy since he was left on my property. Plus he seems a little attached to me. I wish I could adopt himself myself or even just foster him, but it would be really hard to have a dog given the private and group training sessions I also hold in the yard at my house."

Bethany smiled as the dog sat beside Shane, his head practically leaning against Shane's thigh. "I'll just let Birdie know what's going on. Be right back."

He watched her walk away. "Trouble," he whispered to his new furry buddy. "Big-time trouble."

As Bethany came back through the door, now wearing a Furever Paws sweatshirt, he froze, a memory overtaking him. He'd met Bethany because she'd been wearing a Furever Paws sweatshirt. She sat next to him in history class their senior year, but prior to then, they'd never spoken. Mostly because she'd never looked his way. She always kept her head down, pencil in hand, taking notes on whatever the teacher was saying. But that day, he'd noticed the logo and said he was thinking of volunteering there, that he loved dogs. Bethany's smile had practically knocked him off his chair, and he'd been unable to get her off his mind. She would barely respond back when he'd try to make conversation, but slowly, she started opening up. As their friendship developed, she explained that she tended to close herself off because she figured any guy who paid her attention was looking for one thing: to get what her reputation implied she was willing to give. She'd opened up about the truth, that she'd actually never even kissed a guy, and after that, they'd talked about everything, their friendship deepening until he finally asked if he could kiss her. It took her two weeks to say yes. And then *magic*.

He never did get the chance to volunteer there with Bethany his senior year. His family had been blowing up because of his father, and there were money issues. Shane already had a part-time job back then and he'd added hours, giving most of his paycheck to his dad. But Shane hadn't fully understood that he was throwing the money away. That realization came later.

"We're gonna take you to get checked over by the nicest vet," Bethany said to the dog. "And he's just down the hall. But first, let's take you outside in the yard."

Good idea. Strays could be nervous about getting on the veterinarian's table and being poked and prodded, so a little time outside in a safe fenced-in area with them would help him feel more comfortable.

The pooch tilted his head and looked at her, and they both smiled.

Outside, in the dog run with the trees providing lots of good smells of chipmunks and squirrels, the dog chased after the ball Shane threw, proudly dropping it at his feet. Shane threw it again, too aware of Bethany beside him. The golden highlights in her pretty brown hair. The lack of a ring on her left hand. Her light, floral perfume. Memories of their first kiss hit him hard—that had been a very emotional moment for her. As was when they'd lost their virginity to each other in a tent they'd worked hard to make very romantic deep in the woods.

"So how did you end up working with dogs?" Bethany asked, shaking him from that beautiful remembrance.

"The summer after graduation, my household basically blew up. My dad walked out. I knew things were getting bad financially because I overheard some nasty arguments between my parents, but I didn't know how bad—and neither did my mom. We were bankrupt."

"Oh, Shane, I'm so sorry. I do remember you talking about your family having to watch finances."

He nodded. "My dad gambled away all the money

I gave him every week from my paycheck. He'd long since spent my college fund too. So there went those plans. I figured I could put myself through community college and get myself to medical school somehow, some way, but with my dad gone and my mother working two jobs and in one hell of a state between losing her husband and almost losing the house, I had to put college aside to help."

"I can't imagine the stress you were under," she said, her voice full of emotion. "I wish I could have been there for you."

He froze, ball poised in the air, but he dropped his arm. The dog went to explore a good scent. "Why weren't you, Bethany? Why did you just up and leave like that?" Finally, the question he'd wanted the answer to for twelve years.

"I didn't want to interfere with your dreams and plans," she said, looking down at the ground.

"What?" he asked, staring at her.

"The morning after graduation, your mother paid me a visit. You should have seen her face as she glanced around our apartment above the bar. She said, 'Look around, Bethany. This is who you are. This is who your mother is. Six months of dating you and suddenly Shane is talking about getting a full-time job instead of going to college.'" She sucked in a breath. "She told me if I really cared about you, I'd let you fulfill your dreams, be what you were meant to be. And not fall into some low-level job in town and end up married with a kid before you were nineteen. She went on and on, Shane."

He closed his eyes, then dropped his head back. "Jesus Christ, Bethany. I'm so sorry. I had no idea she did that."

Suddenly, Bethany's cold phone call made sense. She hadn't left him out of nowhere. She'd been manipulated out of town by his mother. For *nothing*.

Good riddance to bad rubbish, he once again recalled his mother saying when she asked him why he looked so down that day. He'd told her off, in a way he never had before or since. Their relationship had never fully recovered, not that they'd been particularly close before that. He wondered how things might have gone if he'd known she was the reason for Bethany fleeing town. They very likely would have no relationship at all. He shook his head. He had one mother. And that mother had one child. A piece of him was grateful he *hadn't* known.

"It was a long time ago," Bethany said. "But yeah, it almost killed me. Walking away from you was the hardest thing I'd ever been through. And I'd been through some stuff," she added with a harsh laugh.

He reached over and took her hand. "I'm so damned sorry. Things were bad for my mother back then, not that it's any excuse. She really went off a cliff, emotionally speaking."

"Well, the bright side is that you ended up finding your true passion and so did I," Bethany said. "You were about to tell me how that happened when we got off track."

Better topic. Easier, anyway. "One of my jobs that summer was a dog walking business, and I found I was really good at training dogs on these walks. I made a name for myself just through that, and suddenly, folks were hiring me as a trainer. Word of mouth spread about my success rate and I was unexpectedly making a mint and very busy. So I opened Barkyard Boarding on a huge piece of land out in Kingdom Creek, and when I got married, my wife and I built a house on the property. When the business got too big for even my yard, I bought a building in town and moved the facility there."

"Is it hard to live alone in Kingdom Creek now—whenever Wyatt isn't with you?" she asked.

"It felt very strange in the beginning. Nina and I got married because she was pregnant. We'd only been dating a few months and really didn't know each other. But we both wanted to make it work for the baby's sake—and we tried, hard. She told me she knew we'd made a mistake by the time she was nine months along. So you can imagine how unhappy we both were, how mismatched. We split truly amicably, making fair custody arrangements. Sometimes the short marriage feels like a dream, like it didn't really happen. Except there's Wyatt to assure me it did."

"Where is that little cutie, by the way?" Bethany asked.

"My neighbor Sally watches him when I need a sitter. She has two young grandchildren, but they live far away and she adores Wyatt. I'm very lucky to have her."

"How's your mom as a sitter?" she asked, eyebrow raised.

"Actually, she's terrific. Grandmother of the year. Doting, loving, actually follows Nina's long list of rules, even when my mother doesn't agree with them."

"That's good," Bethany said, turning away to watch the dog.

It helped a lot, that was for sure. Anna Dupree was a great grandmother and she'd been there for Nina from the get-go, even though she didn't like her much either.

Shane sighed, mentally shaking his head.

"Well, let's get this sweetheart checked out," Bethany said. He could hear the strain in her voice. The trip outside had gotten a little more intense than either had expected.

"Mikey," Shane called out, dropping to one knee. "Hey, Mikey. Got something for ya." He held out a treat, and the dog came bounding over. "Good, boy!"

"I don't know why he's Mikey, but he is." He gave the pooch a reassuring pat.

Bethany smiled. "Mikey it is."

A half hour later, Doc J had given Mikey a clean bill of health, along with his necessary shots and the usual monthly meds—heartworm and flea and tick preventative. The stray had no microchip, so Bethany explained that Furever Paws would put notices about him on local "lost dog" sites. If no one claimed him after five days, the rescue would list him for adoption once he was assessed and given the green light.

Shane wasn't quite ready to part ways with Bethany yet. Bad sign. But he just couldn't feel any urgency to leave. Sally, his ace sitter, had taken Wyatt to the park to see the ducks. It was such a gorgeous early spring day that they probably wouldn't be back home for another hour at least.

"How about a warm bath, Mikey?" Bethany asked the dog as they left the clinic. "You'll smell just a bit like lavender, and no one will be able to resist you. The waiting list to adopt you will be miles long."

Shane smiled. "I'll help. I've got a little time before Wyatt's expected home from the park."

Bethany smiled. "You have a real soft spot for Mikey, don't you?"

Yes. And for you, too.

Which scares the hell out of me.

In the grooming room, Shane hoisted Mikey into the tub, and the moment the pooch felt the gentle warm spray, he perked right up. He seemed to love his bath. And man, did he look—and smell—great afterward.

"Just wait till he has on his spiffy blue bandana to denote that he's ready for adoption," Bethany said as they walked Mikey to the kennel room. "He'll find his forever home in no time."

"No doubt," Shane said, his heart feeling three times bigger after all Bethany had done for the too-skinny timid shepherd mix.

"Birdie gave me the rundown of the dogs that are here. They're the ones who aren't ready for foster homes for various reasons." She stopped in front of Meatball's kennel. Beside it was an empty one. "Let's put Mikey next to this wonderful friend."

Shane peered in at the basset hound. He barely lifted his head. "Aw, he's shy, huh?"

"And hard to place. He's a senior and needs a weight loss regimen. But he's such a sweetheart. I just met him today and I'm already smitten."

"I guess a house about to be renovated is no place

for a shy basset hound," Shane said. It was too bad. He could tell she really adored the pooch. But then, she'd always loved dogs. "I'm surprised you don't have a dog of your own."

"I've fostered in the past," she said. "Often, actually. But when it's time to hand over the dog to its forever owner, I do. I keep my heart out of it."

"How?" He could use tips on that last part—where Bethany was concerned.

She glanced away. "Long-term training, I guess. From life. I don't let myself fall in love. I'm a lone wolf like I've always been. No husband, no kids, no pets."

Except he could hear the strain in her voice. "Sounds lonely, though."

"I wouldn't know otherwise," she said quickly, then knelt down to open the kennel door for Mikey.

His heart clenched. She *had* known otherwise. During their time together. Granted, it was just six months a long time ago, but what they'd had had been special. Then again, given the way his mother had run her out of town, away from him, he could see why she'd closed herself off. And since she didn't have a ring on or a significant other with her, it seemed that relationships hadn't worked out since.

"Well, I'd better get to work!" she said too brightly.

"See you at seven?" he asked. "At the house. Oh, and give me your number. That way, if I'm running late or something, I can text to let you know." She complied, and he entered her number into his phone, shooting her a smile when he was done. "Great, see you at seven. I'll bring power tools and a pizza."

Pizza. That sounded very...friendly. Too friendly, maybe. She hesitated, then found herself nodding. "With the unexpected new job, I'll need all the help I can get, and I can never turn down pizza."

"With spinach and green peppers?" he asked. "I'm still a pepperoni guy—plus extra cheese."

They shared a lot of pizza way back when. The sweet memory of their tradition of always taking a bite of a slice of the other's half sent goose bumps across her nape. "Yup," she said. "Still my favorite toppings." She cleared her throat. "I'll call the house flipper you mentioned—Harris Vega—and hopefully he can get started right away."

Right away. Lone wolf. No husband, no kids, no pets. She couldn't have made it clearer that she was here till the house was ready to put on the market, then she'd drive off—again.

For his sake, for Wyatt's sake—because no baby needed a dad distracted by a woman who wasn't sticking around...again—he'd be more like Bethany and keep *his* heart out of it.

Chapter Four

Bethany unlocked the front door of The House and poked her head in. Just a house. No ghosts. No creepy-crawlies. *You'll be fine*, she told herself. *You've handled harder than this*. What was that old joke? *I've had steaks tougher than you*. This house wouldn't defeat her, make her anxious, make her sad, or run her out of town. She had to stay here for the time being, but she could deal with that. And besides, this place would soon look very different.

All that said, the moment she stepped inside, her stomach churned. Her gaze landed on the fireplace mantel, which held a few knickknacks but no photographs. She glanced around, realizing there wasn't much in the way of personal touches to the place. Good.

She headed into the living room, avoiding looking at the recliners, and dropped her purse on the coffee table. *This is home for the next few weeks, so you might as well make it as okay for yourself as possible*. She went upstairs to check out the guest room, where she'd be sleeping. As she walked past the master bedroom, she closed the door. Down the hall she found a decent-sized bedroom with a queen bed, dresser with mirror, a braided rug, and a rocking chair with a cushion by the window. There was a framed photograph of the seashore on one wall. It looked like the kind of nice but bland room you'd get at a hotel, and that suited her just fine. She grabbed the bedding—pillowcases, sheets, and the comforter—then realized she has no idea where the washer and dryer were. Perhaps on this level. She opened a set of closets near the hall bathroom and bingo. Two big machines. She stuffed in the sheets and pillowcases, added some detergent and pressed the start button. The comforter would be next. She felt better about being here already.

Her phone pinged with a text. Forgot to mention I'll be bringing a very cute 18-pound assistant. He can help me make a list of what needs to be done. See you in a few.

So that was Shane's number, apparently. She saved it in her contacts, then texted back a great, see you soon, and maybe it *was* great. Seeing Shane in full dad mode would help her stop thinking about him so much. Package deal. Two Duprees. Double the heartache when something would get in their way. And she had no doubt something would. His mother wouldn't have influence over her anymore, of course, but twelve years of life had certainly changed both her and Shane. He wasn't the same guy he had been at eighteen, and she wasn't the same girl. There was no going back to pick up where they left off. There was only now. And *now*, they were two different people, with lives headed in different directions.

When the doorbell rang at exactly 7:00 p.m., she practically jumped. She opened the door. Shane stood there, looking gorgeous, a pizza box precariously balanced on the basket under Wyatt's stroller seat.

"Ba!" Wyatt said with a big gummy smile.

Bethany laughed. "Ba back at ya!" she said. He sure was cute. A mini Shane. She held the door open and Shane walked in, carefully pushing the stroller.

"Ah, something to put on the list," he said, his gaze on the entryway faceplate, which was hanging down on one side. He pulled his phone out of his pocket and tapped away. "Notes app," he explained. "I already listed that the front door needs a new screen and fresh coat of paint. The walls all needed painting, but Harris will take care of that, along with the kitchen and bathrooms."

She and the house flipper had played phone tag today and it was her turn to call back. She hoped she got him this time. "While you look around and make your list, I'll go call him," Bethany said, already needing to escape Shane and how he filled up the entire foyer. Him and that very cute, sweet baby. She went into the kitchen and pulled up Harris Vega's number again, tapping her fingers on the cracked countertop.

This time, Harris answered on the first ring, which Bethany appreciated. There were times when she prayed she'd get someone's voice mail and times when she hoped the person would answer. For a conversation like this, she was more than happy to avoid another round of phone tag. She explained that she'd inherited a house in need of work but was on a very strict budget.

"Oh, I know Elliot's house," Harris said. "He actually had me over to talk about doing some updating but in the end, he said he didn't want to change the past. So the pink bathroom and outdated kitchen stayed."

Bethany scowled. What she would give to "change the past." Her ridiculous reputation and what it cost her. Shane's mother's disdain and how she'd guilted

Bethany into leaving him. The loneliness and heart-break of those first couple of years on her own, trying to find that soft place to land. Luckily she had—at the animal shelter in Berryville that needed a "hard worker who loved animals and didn't mind real grunt work." That grunt work—cleaning out kennels, scooping litter boxes, handwashing food and water bowls, endless loads of laundry of blankies and stuffed toys—had given her physical work to do, keeping her mind clear. And all those dogs and cats had kept her company and made her feel less alone.

"I was there just a few months ago," Harris continued, "so I know what I'm dealing with. And I'll make you a deal. I'll do good work on a budget for a percentage of the selling price." He named a fair percentage and Bethany agreed.

She wasn't used to things going her way lately. Not having to front any money was a huge relief. "Thank you so much, Mr. Vega."

"Harris. I'm just finishing a job today, and I was supposed to get out of town for a few days but it fell through," he added. "So my schedule is clear, and I can actually start the day after tomorrow. How about if I come over 7:00 a.m. on Wednesday and we'll go over what you want done. I start early. Hope that's okay."

"Perfect, actually." And it was, since her new job hours were officially eight to five, which really meant earlier in the morning and later in the evening as needed. And she'd be needed. "I can't thank you enough."

When she went back in the living room, she told Shane the good news. "And he can start the day after tomorrow."

"Then it's time to celebrate with pizza," he said, pocketing his phone. "Wyatt had a little bit of scrambled eggs and his favorite veggie medley baby food for dinner, almost as good as pizza. So where do you want to eat? Living room? Kitchen?"

"Definitely the kitchen," she said. "The window looks out onto the backyard and all those trees with their tiny buds. Reminder that it's spring."

"And not a minute too soon. Princess hates the cold. If it's under fifty degrees, my mother wants her in her embarrassing, frilly sweaters."

Bethany laughed. She could just see Shane walking down the street with Princess all decked out in a sparkly pink sweater. "It's sweet how she dotes on the dog."

"Oh, it's something all right," he said, rolling his eyes. He wheeled the stroller into the kitchen, Wyatt batting at the mobile on the side before he let out a big yawn. "I think one of your dinner guests is going to fall asleep on you in about twenty minutes."

"Look at those big blue eyes," she said as Wyatt

widened them, clearly trying to stay awake. "They're just like yours." She couldn't get over how utterly precious the baby was. As a child and young teen-ager, she'd made a firm decision never to marry, never to have kids because of her upbringing. But then falling in love with Shane had changed all that. Anything seemed possible then. But the lonely years after, the failed relationships, had her back to her old pronouncements. No family for her. She was long done with heartbreak. Babies sure were sweet, though. She could admit that, even if she knew she'd never have one of her own.

Shane smiled, grabbing the pizza box from atop the basket. "He's definitely my mini-me."

Bethany rummaged through the cabinets, which felt weird, and took out two gold-rimmed dinner plates. She found paper napkins in another cabinet.

"I brought sodas," he said. "I wasn't sure what's in the fridge."

She glanced over at it. The refrigerator had to be thirty years old. "I haven't even opened it yet. I'll clean it out later."

He unscrewed the cap of his soda, and when she did the same, he held up the bottle. "To getting through."

She gaped at him and then laughed. "That's your toast? Your sage words?"

"The right ones, wouldn't you say?" he asked, picking up a slice of pepperoni.

"Oh definitely." She smiled and took a slice of her veggie pizza. "I like your raw honesty, Shane. I like when people talk to me straight."

"Well, if you don't mind a direct question, then can I ask—how's it been, being here in the house? Is it weird?" he asked, taking a bite of his pizza. The extra cheese stretching from the slice to his mouth had her staring at his lips.

"Not too bad," she said. "I'll be staying in the guest room, and it's perfectly fine. I guess at some point I'll need to go into the master bedroom and Elliot's home office and root around to get things sorted and packed up. But not tonight."

"I can imagine how strange that'll feel," he said.

"Very strange. At least there are no family photos in the living room. There's really nothing personal out at all. Maybe he packed all that away when he knew he was getting sick or something."

"He died of a heart attack, actually," Shane said. "Very sudden."

"Oh. How awful." She put her pizza down. "So maybe he just wasn't a sentimental person. I mean, how could he be when he was married and carrying on an affair?"

"He packed up all the framed photos of himself and his wife about a month ago," Shane said.

Bethany paused, pizza midway to her mouth. "Are you sure?" How could Shane know something like that?

"Completely. I was walking Princess for my mother, and he waved me over to ask my help in opening a pickle jar. We were in the kitchen when he burst into tears all of a sudden."

"He did?" Bethany put her pizza down.

"He got all embarrassed, but I assured him it was okay to let it all out and he just stood there, crying, his face buried in a kitchen towel. He dried his eyes and said he was just overwhelmed by the losses—first 'his dear friend,' as he'd put it, Kate Robeson, and then his wife less than a year later. He said he packed up all the photos of him and his wife because he was overwhelmed by his emotions and didn't want reminders of 'not living an honest life.' His words."

Part of Bethany felt for the man. Sobbing in his kitchen. Suddenly all alone. But then she'd picture her mother, sneaking off late at night. Leaving her young daughter with a parade of uninterested sitters. Elliot making a fool of his wife. For more than twenty years. All while enjoying his standing in town as a respected, successful attorney.

Bethany quickly took a bite of her pizza before she

lost her appetite again. "I wonder if he felt guilty about cheating on his wife or for letting my mother be the 'other woman,' despite what it did to her and my reputations. He had to know what people thought of us."

"If you want to know what I think, Bethany, I think Elliot was deeply in love with your mother and that ruled him. I'm not excusing him. Just trying to explain how he saw things."

Bethany stared at him. "So why not end his marriage and marry my mother? People *do* get divorced. People *do* remarry. Who carries on an affair for decades?"

"That day when he cried, he said he promised his wife years back that he'd never leave her, and that she gave him permission to do what he wanted as long as he was discreet."

"I don't want to talk about this," she said, her chest feeling tight and hollow at the same time.

He reached his hand out and squeezed hers. How good that felt. His warm, strong hand. If she wasn't so self-controlled, she'd fling herself into his arms. A hug from Birdie had been wonderful, but to be in Shane's arms, her head against that rock-hard chest, was all she wanted right now.

Wyatt let out another giant yawn, and they both turned to him, Shane's hand slipping from hers.

Bethany could barely smile at the sweet baby boy.

How had she gotten here? Literally and figuratively. Twelve years ago, she'd thought she was going to marry Shane. After college. They'd live in medical school housing, and then after his residency, they'd have a baby, even though the idea scared her. Now she was sitting in the house Elliot left her—either out of a lack of options or because she was his child—with Shane Dupree, whose life, like hers, hadn't gone according to plan. Except for the baby. A baby he'd had with someone else.

"Do you think Elliot left me the house because I *am* his daughter?" Bethany asked. "Did he say anything about that?"

"He never mentioned you to me," Shane said. "I don't think he even knew we were together once. I mean, it was just six months and you only came over to my house a couple times."

Just six months. Those six months had changed her world, her life. "Your mother was ice-cold to me. I'm surprised I actually came more than once."

"I'm sorry, Bethany. For everything you went through. It was so damned unfair."

She looked at him, then turned away. "When Elliot's lawyer called me, he said Elliot told him he was claiming me as his daughter. That's different from admitting he's my father."

"Do you believe he is?" Shane asked.

She shrugged. "I've gone back and forth on it. My mother told me that she did date a lot—until she met Elliot. Then she was in love. She stopped seeing her other boyfriends. I came along soon after. We never talked about it, but I got the sense that she wasn't sure who the dad was. DNA testing thirty years ago wasn't the easy big thing it is now."

Shane let out a sigh. "Maybe you'll find proof in the house, one way or another. Documents or something. In his home office."

"I thought about that on the drive up to Spring Forest. But maybe I don't want to know."

"How could you not?" he asked.

"Because I already hate that my mother loved a cheater. For twenty-five years she loved a cheating bastard. Do I really want to claim that man as my father?"

"Maybe there was more to him than that, Bethany."

"Nope," she said, lifting her chin.

"Well, I'm stepping into territory I have no business in," he said. "You had three bites of your pizza. Let's eat and maybe talk about something that won't put your stomach in knots. Like Mikey. Think he and Meatball are talking through their kennels? Swapping stories about where they came from, how they got here?"

She smiled, though tears were stinging the backs of her eyes. "I hope they are. I really do."

He reached out his hand again. "You're going to get through this, Bethany Robeson. You're a strong person, full of grit and determination. And I'm here for you, okay?"

She *was* strong. She *did* have grit. She *was* determined. But she wasn't so sure that Shane Dupree suddenly being "there for her" was something she could handle. How could she let herself count on someone when she already knew how much it would hurt her to let him go? Last time, it almost destroyed her. "I guess that toast we clinked to really was the right one."

He squeezed her hand, then let go and stood up. "Well, I'd better get the sleepyhead home. He can barely keep his eyes open."

She didn't want them to leave. And not because she didn't want to be alone in the house.

His phone pinged and he pulled it out, frowning as he read the screen.

"Everything okay?" she asked.

"Sally—the neighbor who watches Wyatt—just let me know she can't sit for Wyatt tomorrow morning during my early training class. Her daughter's ill, so she's leaving for a few days to care for her grandkids."

"I'm not due at Furever Paws till 8:00 a.m.," she heard herself saying before she even thought about it—on any level. "I can watch him till 7:45. Will that help?"

Wasn't her goal to keep her *distance*? But on the other hand, the whole reason he was here was to help *her* out. How could she not return the favor when he needed one?

His smile made her knees all trembly. "The class ends at 7:45, so that would be perfect. I teach the early morning class in my actual backyard at the house, not at Barkyard Boarding," he said. "It's the staff's busiest time with walking and feeding the boarders, so I like the quiet calm of my Kingdom Creek property during that time. I'll text you the address—could you come at 6:30?" He got Wyatt settled in his stroller, the little guy letting out another giant yawn as his blue eyes drooped. "If you're sure it's no trouble."

Bethany walked them to the door. "No trouble at all. See you then."

But of course it was trouble. Big trouble. Because Bethany was falling for Shane Dupree all over again.

When Shane and Wyatt left, Bethany remembered she hadn't put the clean wash in the dryer and went upstairs to do that and stuff the comforter in the washer. Because her head was about to explode from the entire day's emotional roller coaster, she bent down and looked through the round glass window at the sheets and pillowcases going round and round.

Had she volunteered to babysit for Shane's son? Yes, she had. So she had to get through her first night in this house, wake up and head to Shane's, and then start her new job. A lot of *new* right there. Bethany wasn't used to new. She liked knowing what to expect. But she could kiss any kind of comfort zone goodbye.

Wyatt's just a baby, she told herself. *Just like this house is just a house. You'll be fine. You might be babysitting the son of the man you loved more than anything, the man you cannot allow yourself to get involved with while you're here, but you can handle this as long as you remember that it is all temporary.* Not to mention, it felt very make-believe. Like it couldn't possibly be real. Shane back in her life? Staying in Elliot Bradley's house? Watching Wyatt Dupree—and very likely having to hold him in her arms?

Go do something and stop thinking, she told herself. She went out to her car and got her big suitcase. She'd packed only a week's worth of clothes, figuring she wouldn't be here past that, but at least she'd brought a few nice outfits that would be suitable for Furever Paws—director-nice but also animal-shelter friendly, meaning nothing white and definitely nothing dry-clean only. As she lugged the suitcase to the house, she glanced over at the Dupree home, wondering how Princess was doing all by her lonesome. Maybe she'd text Shane to ask if she should go check on the Chihuahua once before she went to bed.

Maybe.

Or maybe she was getting a little too involved in the man's life.

She had a while before the laundry would be done and she could settle into bed. She supposed she could take a look around, poke her head in rooms, see what she was dealing with, how much packing up and clearing out she'd have to do. She'd certainly need to get a lot of it done before Harris Vega started the renovations. His work would be easier if there wasn't a lot of junk in his way.

She went into the kitchen and began opening drawers. Utensils, plates, glasses, pantry foods. The refrigerator didn't contain much—milk, orange juice, butter, some neatly stacked Tupperware containers. She'd clear it all out tomorrow after work and go grocery shopping.

Elliot's office was in the hallway between the kitchen and living room. A large, masculine room with a big cherry desk and matching chair with a black cushion. She opened one of the side drawers. Office supplies. Bottom drawer, files.

Tax returns. Utilities. Property taxes. Charitable contributions.

Kate Robeson.

Bethany Robeson.

Bethany almost jumped backward. A file with her name on it? Maybe it had something to do with leaving her the house. The deed, that kind of thing. Or maybe, like Shane had said, there was some documentation about her paternity.

She shut the drawer.

Then opened it again.

How could you want to know something and *not* want to at the same time?

She stared at the file with her mother's name. She couldn't imagine what was in there. Love letters? Photographs?

Too much. Too much for one day—and her first day back in town, at that. Staying at the house and having dinner with the Dupree boys was already enough to have her mind in a whirl. She couldn't take any more. A good night's sleep and maybe tomorrow night after work she'd feel ready to look inside those files.

Or maybe not.

Chapter Five

The next morning, Shane cleared the breakfast dishes, pleased with how the meal had gone. Wyatt was trying more and more solid foods these days, and it was fun to watch him pick up the tiny pieces of soft scrambled egg and put them in his mouth. Wyatt loved scrambled eggs. Soon enough, Shane would be making them both he-man omelets with everything imaginable stuffed inside. Not that he was trying to speed up time. He'd long heard how fast childhood went; you blinked, and your kid was graduating from high school. Shane couldn't even imagine. He didn't want to miss a second of it.

He glanced at the time glowing on the microwave and took a long drink of his coffee. Six forty-two. Bethany would be here any minute.

"Better make up your bottle," Shane told Wyatt.

"Ba!" was his response, followed by a fit of giggles.

"I agree that *ba* is very funny," Shane said, grinning at his son.

The doorbell rang just as Shane set the bottle on the counter. Bethany had arrived. As he ushered her back into the kitchen, he saw that she'd come bearing two take-out cups of coffee and a small bag from Whole Bean Coffee.

"Light and sweet for the coffee and a corn muffin," she said, holding up the bag. "Or at least you used to love corn muffins."

He remembered how she liked her coffee too. Cream, one sugar. "Still do," he said. He peered in the bag and took a piece of the muffin and popped it in his mouth. "Ah, delicious. Love Whole Bean treats. And thanks, by the way." He took a sip of the coffee, then another. "Perfect."

She smiled and took a sip of her own coffee.

"I've only got a few minutes before I need to head out back to greet the early birds," he said. "I've got Wyatt's bottle all ready," he said, gesturing to where he'd left it on the counter. "Mind giving it to him?"

She stared at him for a moment, and he could see

her thinking it over. "Not at all. It would be a first, though. I've never fed a baby before."

"Me either, before Wyatt came along. So I only have seven months more experience than you. It's easy-peasy. He'll let you know when he's done."

She bit her lip. "I'm not even sure I know how to hold a baby to feed him. Positioning, I mean."

"I'll show you," he said. "In fact, why don't we go out on the deck. It's a gorgeous morning, unusually warm for March. You guys can sit out there or stay inside, whichever you prefer."

"Outside sounds good. And I can watch your class."

He wet a paper towel and then walked over to Wyatt, cleaning the bits of egg off his hands and face before getting him out of the high chair. Bethany was right behind him.

"Hi, cutie," she said. "I'll be keeping you company while your daddy is teaching the class."

"Here," Shane said, slightly holding out his arms. "Why don't you take him out to the deck, and I'll bring the bottle and his stroller so you can pop him in at any time."

The transfer went well, Wyatt going easily into Bethany's arms, his big blue eyes riveted on her face. Yup, Shane thought, agreeing, she's hard to look away from.

"I think he likes me!" Bethany said, running the back of a finger down Wyatt's cheek. The baby really was staring at her. He reached out and grabbed her chin.

"Ba!" Wyatt said.

"Is *Ba* your favorite word?" Bethany asked. "I like it too."

"It's all he babbles so far," Shane said, heading toward the stroller in the hallway. He wheeled it toward the sliding glass doors in the family room, stopping to grab the bottle. "I can't wait for him to talk, but I don't want to rush anything, you know?"

"Totally," she said.

Bethany Robeson holding his son. The image of her standing by the sliding glass door, Wyatt in her arms, making cute faces at him as he stared up at her in wonder, would stay with him for a long time.

Out on the deck in the gorgeous spring weather—already sixty degrees so early—Bethany carefully sat on the cushioned love seat.

"So just recline him a bit against your upper arm," he said. He watched as Bethany repositioned Wyatt a little. "Perfect. Now you can hold the bottle for him and he'll hold it too—he's just starting to be able to hold it himself, but when it's full it's heavy for him."

Wyatt started happily drinking, content as could be, the breeze playing in his brown hair.

"Wow," she said, gazing down at the baby. "Feeding a baby is kind of magical."

"Sure is," he said. "I used to be so afraid I'd drop him his first couple of weeks on earth."

"Should I be honest and tell you I'm scared to death I *will* drop him? He feels so sturdy, though. Fragile but solid at the same time."

"You just described parenthood," he said with a grin.

She bit her lip, watching the baby, repositioning the bottle as needed.

And he watched her, unable to tear his gaze away. Bethany, holding, feeding his baby son. Unbelievable.

"Your training field is so nice," she said, and he was suddenly aware of how close he was to her, that he should put some space between them. She glanced down at Wyatt, then back out at where he had a good-sized loop for practicing leash walking and heeling and basic commands. There were several outdoor dog beds and filled water bowls. He usually only held the early morning class here, but he liked having the training area as a backup. The entire yard was fenced.

"Hi, Shane!" a voice called out.

Shane turned to see Michael Drumm and his recently rescued Lab mix, Moxie, entering through the side gate.

"You go ahead," Bethany said. "I think I've got the hang of this. But don't leave the yard or anything!"

"I won't, newbie," he said, smoothing Wyatt's hair. He shot her a smile, then headed out to greet Michael and Moxie. In the next minute, one of his employees, Dylan, who wanted to specialize in dog training, had arrived to assist, and the rest of the class of twelve students and their pooches streamed in, hellos and sniffs as everyone got into place.

Shane did a mental rundown of the attendees and their dogs. Everyone was accounted for, but there was someone new, with a dog he'd never seen before. The class was full and so registration was closed. What Shane had here, he figured, was a sneak-in. A pint-size sneak-in.

"No, Pickles," the boy, about nine years old, whispered to the small gray terrier mix beside him, who was currently chasing his tail. "Pickles, stop that."

Pickles did not stop that.

Shane recognized the kid. Danny McJones lived next door, but given the size of Shane's lot, next door was a good quarter mile away. "Okay, folks, I want you to practice walking and heeling, like we learned last week. Dylan will lead you around the loop. Keep ten feet from the person and dog in front of you to give your furry friend his or her own space."

As the group started to head over to the loop, Shane walked over to Danny and Pickles, now digging a hole in Shane's backyard.

"No, Pickles," Shane said in a firm voice. The dog stopped and looked at him. Shane reached into his pocket for a high-value treat from his various baggies. Holding the treat in front of the dog's nose, Shane slowly moved it over Pickles's head, toward his rear and said, "Sit!" As the dog's eyes followed the treat, he sat. "Yes," Shane said, immediately giving Pickles the treat. "Good boy!"

"Wow, you *are* good!" Danny said. "Just like I heard. That's why I came today. We adopted Pickles a week ago, but my dad says we have to give him back to Furever Paws. Pickles doesn't listen at all and chewed up my dad's work shoes. And he peed on the new rug my mom just bought." Danny's hazel eyes filled with tears. "My dad says we don't have the time or money to hire a trainer and that we need to get a well-behaved, calm dog instead."

"Is that why you're here? So you and Pickles can take the training class?"

Danny nodded. "I can only stay a half hour, though, then I have to bring Pickles home and make it to the school bus. If we're both quiet, can we stay?"

"Do your parents know you're here?" Shane asked.

The mop of brown hair swung back and forth. "No, I snuck out."

"Tell you what, Danny. Why don't you and Pickles go join the group. You can just practice walking with Pickles on a leash for right now, okay? I'll be over in a minute."

"You're gonna call my house, aren't you?" the boy said with a scowl.

"Yup. Go ahead now." He reached into his baggie and pulled out three treats. "Every time Pickles does what you want, even just walking nicely beside you, give him a treat and say 'Good, Pickles!' in a happy voice. If he doesn't do what you want, say 'No, Pickles' in a firm voice and don't give him a treat."

Danny's frown immediately turned upside down. "C'mon, Pickles, I'm training you!"

Shane walked over to the deck where Bethany was sitting and pulled out his phone.

"Aww," Bethany said, shifting Wyatt in her arms as he continued to drink from his bottle. "One of the top three reasons a dog is returned to a shelter is because he's not 'perfect' in the first week." Apparently, she'd heard the whole thing. Bethany shook her head. "I'm always grateful when people adopt, but I wish they wouldn't rush to judgment. They have to give it a chance. And working on training is a must. Now a kid is going to be heartbroken."

"I feel for him," Shane said. "But I definitely have to call his folks."

Shane looked up the McJones in his Contact list. He had all his neighbors listed, just in case there were dog escapees to report or issues with barking. Ah, there it was. Andrew and Kate McJones.

Kate answered, relieved to hear Danny was safe. She'd been out looking for him and Pickles for the past ten minutes and had gotten increasingly worried when she couldn't find them anywhere. She promised that she and her husband would be over to pick them up in a few minutes even though Shane said he could stay till it was time for the bus.

"Pickles isn't doing too bad," Bethany said, her gaze on the little terrier who was zigzagging on the loop but mostly going in the right general direction. "Danny just has to teach him to stay at his side."

Shane watched the boy, smiling as Danny said, "Good, Pickles!" and gave him a treat when the dog walked two steps on his right side.

The McJones arrived, Andrew calling Danny over while Kate apologized to Shane for Danny crashing the class.

"He's doing a great job with training Pickles at leash walking," Shane said. "I'm more than willing to help Danny train Pickles—no charge. He can come over a couple times a week after school, and I'll work with them both."

"Really?" Andrew asked.

"Sure. I remember being his age and falling for a stray who didn't know any commands, couldn't walk on a leash without pulling. I was so afraid my parents would make me take him to a shelter. But I promised I'd research training and would work really hard at it, and they said yes. Bucky turned into a great dog and I actually got an entire career out of it. My days off are Thursdays and Fridays. If he wants to come those days after school, I'd be happy to work with them both."

"Danny," Andrew called again, waving him over.

Danny and Pickles came running. "I have to give him back to the shelter, right?" Tears filled his eyes, and Shane could see he was working hard at blinking them back.

"Mr. Dupree has offered to work with you and Pickles after school on Thursdays and Fridays. Are you willing to work hard at learning how to train Pickles? You'll need to practice what you learn every day."

"Yes!" Danny shouted. "We'll work really hard, right, Pickles?"

Pickles gave a little bark.

"Well, there's our answer," Shane said. "It's a deal then. I'll see you tomorrow after school, Danny. Three thirty. Have a snack at home, leash up Pickles and come on over."

"Awesome!" Danny said.

The McJoneses thanked him at least five more times, then they had to get Danny to school.

He and Bethany watched them disappear around the side of the house.

"You're a very generous person," Bethany said. "But I already knew that."

"Eh, I was nine once. And besides, you don't want Pickles next to Meatball and Mikey at Furever Paws. The objective is a forever home—not a return to the kennels."

Her smile almost made his knees shake.

"Wyatt's all done with his bottle," she said, setting it on the patio table. "Do I burp him?"

Shane nodded. "Just hold him vertically against you and give him a few pats on his back. Watch your nice outfit, though." He reached into his back pocket and pulled out a burp cloth. He always had one on him.

He watched her ease a big burp out of Wyatt and shot her a thumbs-up. "I'd better get back to the class. See you soon."

As he jogged over to the loop, he turned to see

Bethany giving Wyatt a snuggle, and something inside him shifted, as if room was being made for her inside him. He wasn't sure if that was good or bad, though.

"Hmm," Birdie said as she and Bethany scooped out the food for the dogs at Furever Paws. "You babysat for Shane during his training class at his house, and he's helping you at your house, taking care of the little things. Sounds like you two are really there for each other."

Bethany reached for the can of dog food. "It's just kind of worked out that way. I mean, he did just happen to be coming out of his mom's house when I arrived at Elliot's place. And I was right there when he got the text that his sitter couldn't watch Wyatt this morning."

"You know what my sister Bunny would call that? Fate." Birdie was a major realist, though.

"What do *you* call it?"

Birdie grinned. "Now that I'm in love and happier than I've been in a long time? I call it a sign."

Bethany laughed. "Not quite willing to go all New Age, but getting there, I see."

Birdie patted her hand. "Little by little I do seem to be changing."

"I wouldn't mind changing. Feeling less closed to

things. But everything feels so scary. The reason I inherited the house. Being back here in town. Suddenly having Shane in my life. Holding his baby son. Feeding him. I even *burped* him."

"Shane's as good as they come," Birdie said with a definitive nod. "When the tornado struck, he was out looking for any strays who might need shelter. And when he heard about the damage to the building, he was here in a heartbeat, moving rubble and debris. When I need an assessment of a dog behaviorally, he'll always come and won't charge me. And if I'm shorthanded on volunteers who are able to walk the difficult dogs, there he is."

"He was always a great guy," Bethany said, feeling tears sting her eyes. "But I can't think of him as anything except a friend. What it took to get over him, Birdie... I can't ever go through that again."

They set all the bowls on a big tray and Birdie led the way to the kennels.

"But you can't hide away from the best things in life, either, Bethany. Trusting in people and love is tough, I know that. But being all closed off, saying no to everything and everyone? That's no way to live either."

"Even if I could imagine a second shot, he has a baby and has always wanted a big family. I'm not the right person to give him that. And besides, I'm leaving anyway once the house sells and either Rebekah comes back full time or you find a permanent director."

Birdie sighed. "Bethany, you used to have only one dream in life—leaving Spring Forest. From the first time we met, that was all you looked forward to. But then Shane changed that. And remember, he didn't end things between you two. He must have been as devastated as you were. Don't forget that. Avoiding relationships has become familiar. But maybe the need for that has run its course."

Bethany took that all in, her heart clenching. "Meatball looks hungry," she said, hoping Birdie would go with the subject change as she took the bowl with his name on the label.

Birdie smiled gently. "You remind me of me. The old Birdie. Maybe soon you'll remind me of the new Birdie."

"Well, I loved the old Birdie too, so I'm good with being like her." She was lucky to have Bernadette Whitaker to talk to. All that wisdom, compassion and life experience made her full of good advice, delivered in her usual no-nonsense way. What Birdie said counted. Always had.

Bethany knelt down and opened Meatball's kennel, crawling in and sitting beside his bowl. The kennels were very large and double-sided to give the dogs space to move; the back side opened onto a dog run. "Hey there, Meatball. We have a delicious breakfast for you. We're trying a new low-cal food to get you to a healthy weight. Give it a try."

The dog lifted his head and looked from her to the food bowl, sniffing his way over. He looked at her but didn't eat.

"Go ahead, Meatball," she said. "Enjoy."

She gave him a reassuring pat, and he started to eat.

Birdie came out of the kennel three doors down, where a pit bull mix with tummy issues was on the path to recovery. "You guys seem to have a real bond. You can keep him with you in your office if you'd like."

"Hear that, Meatball? I get to foster you right here. On my lunch break, I'll take you for a nice walk. I know where all the easy inclines are too."

Birdie laughed. "I think Meatball's going to be adoptable very soon."

Once they finished handing out the bowls, Birdie went to her office, and Bethany put Meatball on a leash and led him to her office, then hurried back to pick up his bed, blankie and chew toy, putting it all in the corner across from her desk. He glanced at her shyly, then got in his bed and curled up, his sweet chin on the rim of the yellow bed.

"So you hang out here, Meatball," she said, giving him another pat. "I've got to go run my first staff meeting. See you soon."

A half hour later, Bethany felt even more at home and ready to tackle her new, temporary job. She'd heard from the staff and volunteers on their thoughts about the animals, with them sharing anything she should know, anything they felt needed taking care of. Rebekah Whitaker, who was now working part-time as the assistant director, had come in for the meeting, bringing along her incredibly adorable twins, six-month-old Lily and Lucas. Great-aunt Birdie was watching the twins for Rebekah during the meeting, sitting at the back and keeping on ear on the discussion.

Every time one of the twins let out a fussy noise—which no one minded because they were all so used to very loud barking dogs—Rebekah would turn around and peer with curiosity or worry toward the twins. Bethany understood; it had to be hard to be pulled in two directions, each competing for your attention.

After the meeting, Bethany and Rebekah sat in Bethany's office, Rebekah on the floor beside Meatball, stroking his long, silky ears, and giving her take on the job and what the priorities should be.

"Bethany," Rebekah said, biting her lip and shoving her long brown hair behind her shoulders, "I want you to know upfront that I'm really not sure if I'll ever be coming back full time. I mean, my sister-in-law, Josie Whitaker, moved to town to help us out with babysitting—she's staying with us in our garage apartment and she's wonderful—and leaving those babies is *still* really hard."

"I know it can't be easy leaving your heart at home whenever you have to go somewhere without them."

Rebekah brightened with relief that Bethany seemed to understand. "I get hit with a little judgment from both camps. One side seems to think I should put my career first. The other thinks I should put the twins and motherhood first. I wish I could devote myself to both, but I've tried that and it means dividing my focus and not being fully present for either one."

"I totally understand," Bethany said.

"The thing with running an animal rescue is that it's not just a 'career,' it's a calling and really a 24/7 job."

"It sure is," Bethany said. "Just know that while I'm here, I'll give Furever Paws my best and my whole heart."

"I can already see that in everything you do and

say," Rebekah said. She took a sip of her herbal tea. "Do you have children?"

Bethany shook her head and quickly took a sip of her coffee, not wanting to have to explain herself. But Rebekah seemed to understand.

"Well, I'll let you get to work," Rebekah said. "Need anything, just text me anytime."

"I appreciate that."

As Rebekah left, Bethany heard a familiar male voice.

Shane.

Looking gorgeous and sexy in jeans and a dark blue Henley shirt, Shane gave a tap on the door. "I'm on my way to Barkyard Boarding, but just wanted to see how Mikey was doing and to say thanks for this morning. You saved the day."

Bethany smiled. "Well, I had a lot of fun saving the day. Wyatt is precious and seems like a really easy baby."

"Trust me, he has his moments, but yeah, he's the best."

"And Mikey is doing great. Unfortunately, we haven't had any calls back about the postings we put up on lost-dog sites. Few more days and we'll list him for adoption."

"I'm sure he'll find a great home," he said, turning toward the door. He seemed like he wanted to say something else, but didn't.

Suddenly, there was nothing scheduled for them. No house visit with pizza. No babysitting need. He volunteered at Furever Paws at least once a week, but didn't have a set schedule; he just came when he could. He'd be over some time to take care of the small fixes around the house, but they hadn't set a day or time.

She wasn't sure when she'd see him again. She only knew she *wanted* to.

Chapter Six

At seven thirty that night, Shane pulled into the driveway at his mother's house, his gaze on the colonial next door. Lights were on inside. He wanted to take Wyatt's car seat—the baby was fast asleep—and knock on the door, but he knew he shouldn't. Not if he actually wanted to keep his emotional distance. He'd already dropped by the shelter today. Granted, he did want to see how Mikey was doing and thank Bethany for this morning, but he also wanted to *see* her.

Go take care of Princess like you're supposed to.

He got out of the car, transferring Wyatt's car seat into the stroller so smoothly that the baby didn't make a peep. Shane kept his eyes on his mother's house, the reason for being here, and forced himself up the walk.

He'd been over twice already today to take Princess for a walk. After learning what his mother had done, how she'd broken up him and Bethany, particularly during what was already a terrible time for Shane, he'd had trouble going inside earlier today. The dog was innocent, though, so he'd put on her pink leash and took her on a mile walk, correcting her zigzagging liked he'd do tomorrow with Danny and Pickles. Princess didn't like to be corrected but she liked bacon-flavored treats, so she kept to the left for the last half of the walk. She wasn't a great student, but she'd get there.

He unlocked the front door, expecting the tiny dog to come running, but she didn't. "Princess, time for your final walk of the day." For a very small dog, Princess loved long walks. Shane slowed down for her, let her sniff away, let her stare down squirrels on tree branches. Usually, the prospect of a walk was enough to have her dancing around his feet, but he'd said the magic word and still no Princess. He called her again and looked around for her, leaving Wyatt sleeping in his stroller in the kitchen. He checked the backyard, which she accessed by her doggie door. No Princess, and the fence was escape-proof.

He texted Bethany. Available to help me look for mysteriously missing Princess? Can't find her anywhere.

She texted back seconds later. Be right there.

By the time he walked back to the front door, she was tapping on it. He opened it, his pulse quickening. She was in sexy gray leggings and a long black sweater, her hair in a ponytail, and she carried a mozzarella cheese stick, which few dogs could resist. If he was this drawn by a woman holding cheese, he was more far gone than he thought.

"She's gotta be here somewhere," Bethany said.

Shane went into the kitchen to check on Wyatt. "He's fast asleep and okay where he is for right now. Maybe Princess is hiding upstairs."

As they headed up the stairs, he was aware of Bethany stopping midway up the staircase. She had one hand on the banister, her gaze riveted to the photographs on the wall. They were all of Shane's childhood, quite a few of him as a teenager.

"I very rarely let myself look at photos of you, of us," she said. "I have a bunch of old selfies. But here you are, just as I always remembered you."

"I still have the selfies too." When she first left, when he was his lowest because of how heartbroken he was and his father's betrayal of their family, he'd look at the photos just to remember he'd once been truly happy, that it was possible. It had taken a long time to come back from that dark place. Thinking about it now was a good reminder not to go back there, not to let himself become all entangled with Bethany Robeson again. What had helped him through those hard days: dogs. And now he had a missing one on his hands. "Maybe Princess is hiding in my mom's room."

He went down the hall, stopping in front of the master bedroom, which his mother had slowly redecorated over the past several years. There were few reminders of his father in this house, which they'd saved together.

He went into the frilly room and lowered himself to the floor to look under the bed. Princess was there, chomping on a rawhide bone.

"Did you not hear me call you?" he demanded of the Chihuahua. He stood up and turned to Bethany, who stayed in the doorway. "I think she's sick of being told what to do."

Bethany laughed. "I'll bet."

"Last walk of the night, Princess," he said in a singsong tone. "You know you love our walks."

The Chihuahua stayed put. Fine. He'd resume their training tomorrow.

"Well, I tried," he said.

Bethany bent down, waving the open mozzarella

stick. "Oh, Princess, look what I have for you." She tore off a piece and waved it around.

The dog came bolting over and gobbled the treat out of Bethany's fingers, then flew back under the bed.

Shane laughed. "Smart dog. All right, Princess—" he directed his comment to the bed "—use your doggie door if you have to go out. I'll see you in the morning and we'll work on heeling."

The Chihuahua didn't respond.

He turned off the light and they went back downstairs to the kitchen. Wyatt was still asleep. Shane wheeled the stroller over to the door.

"This place doesn't look anything like I remember," Bethany said, looking around, "but I really wasn't here much, was I? Your mom made it clear I wasn't welcome."

"I've been trying not to think about the conversation I'm going to have with my mother when she comes back from her vacation," he said. "But there'll be one."

What would life have been like had Bethany stayed? They would have gotten married, he had no doubt.

Of course, if life hadn't gone as it had, there would be no Wyatt. And Shane couldn't imagine that.

He let out a breath. "The reason the house doesn't

look familiar is because I helped my mom renovate and redecorate. Get rid of the old memories."

"Ah," she said. "I can relate."

"How's it going next door?"

"I'm getting more and more used to it. I cleaned out the fridge and pantry and restocked. Got a few looks at the grocery store, like 'Is that Bethany Robeson?' And I heard someone say, 'She inherited Elliot Bradley's big house. I always knew she was his kid.'" She shook her head. "It's amazing that anyone remembers me twelve years later or cares about this stuff. But I guess small towns have long memories."

He hated that she had to deal with this crud. C'mon, people.

"Very true," he said. "My family was the talk of the town for years after my dad left. There was plenty of wrong info floating around, but a lot of it right. Hearing the gossip would make me want to punch a wall, but try walking a one-hundred-forty-pound Newfoundland with only one good arm."

She gave him a commiserating smile. "How'd you get through that time?"

"The dogs."

She stared at him for a moment and then just walked very close to him and threw her arms around him. "Me too," she whispered.

He inwardly gasped, wrapping his arms around

her in return. He wasn't expecting to ever have Bethany in his arms again, but now that she was here, her head buried against his chest, it was as though twelve years hadn't slowly gone by.

Memory after memory flashed through his mind. The way they'd walk off into the woods, holding hands on the trail, talking about everything, or sometimes just in silence, their company enough. The first time he'd kissed her. Held her. Made love to her.

He was about to stroke her hair and tell her everything would be okay, but she stepped back.

"Sorry about that," she said. "I got a little overwhelmed."

"By?"

"Once, you and I were so in sync, Shane. We understood each other so well. And just now, with dogs getting us both through the hardest time in our lives, it just seemed kind of…" She trailed off but he got it.

"The same," he said. "The connection."

"Yeah," she whispered. She sucked in a breath and turned away, and he could tell she was trying to collect herself. "I should get back. Harris is coming by early to see the house and give me a time frame on the renovations."

"Sure, I'd love a cup of a coffee," he said with a gentle smile.

She narrowed her eyes and shook her head with a

grin. "How did you get an invitation for coffee out of what I just said? Though I did get a pound of toffee-chocolate coffee beans ground fresh at Whole Bean today and a pumpkin pie from the Great American Bakery."

"I love pumpkin pie," he said.

They both did.

"I feel bad that Wyatt will sleep through the pie," she said. "Not that he can have pie at seven months."

Relief—and something else he couldn't quite put his finger on—came over him. He didn't want her to be alone right now.

And he didn't want to leave her.

That other emotion he'd felt just now? He realized it was nerves-tinged worry. That despite all his efforts to protect himself, he was starting to care about her way too much.

Had she really flung herself into his arms? She had, and she was glad because it felt so damned good. She was grateful he'd invited himself over. She knew that it was less about wanting coffee and more about wanting her to know she had a shoulder to lean on, that she wasn't alone.

She had to stop relying on *his* shoulder, though.

Bethany made a fresh pot of the deliciously scented coffee and cut two slices of pie, bringing the plates over to the table. Wyatt was asleep in his stroller, reclined almost all the way, and for a moment she just ogled his adorableness, his big smooth cheeks, the way his bow lips quirked up occasionally, his little hand curled up by his head.

"Honestly, despite what you used to say, I'm still surprised you don't have one of these of your own," Shane said, almost making her jump. Guess she was caught wistfully staring.

"I knew even as a kid that I wouldn't have kids," she said. "You know that." Even if for the last six months of her senior year, she had been able to see herself as a mother. Love made everything seem bright and shiny and suddenly possible. But when it was gone, Bethany had reverted to her old way of thinking.

"I remember the first time I knew with certainty that I'd never make a child go through what I went through," she said. "I was ten, left with a sitter who ignored me, nothing to eat but bad frozen pizza, no help with homework, upset about something that happened at school and no one to talk to about it. I was confused for a long time about why people talked about my mom." She moved over to the coffee maker to give herself a little privacy in case she got teary, which sometimes happened when she thought about her childhood.

"You had to grow up pretty fast," he said.

"Know what's strange?" she asked. "No matter what, I know my mom loved me. She just wasn't like other moms—in any way, shape or form. And even though I loved her back, I still felt hurt that she'd put me in that situation—that she'd chosen being what her boyfriend needed over being what *I* needed. By the time I was thirteen and understood more, I decided it was better to never have children than to risk my child resenting me like that someday."

"You're allowed to change your mind—you know that, right? A decision you made as a kid, as a teenager can't dictate your future."

"Sure it can," she said. "What would I know about being a good mother? So why risk it?"

He opened his mouth to say something, then bit his lip and said nothing.

"My dad wasn't father of the year," he said. "But I'm trying my best to be the dad I wish I'd had. That's what matters. Not how I was raised."

She brought over the coffee, cream and sugar, her gaze on Wyatt again. "You're a great dad, Shane." *You're just great, period.*

"I appreciate you saying that, but I constantly worry about how I'm doing. I failed at marriage, and what if I fail at this, too?" He stared at Wyatt, his expression grim. "What's more important than being his father?"

"You clearly take that responsibility, that commitment, very seriously. So nothing ever will be more important. I don't think you need to worry one bit."

"I could say the same about you, Bethany. Being a good parent is about being kind, being compassionate, being patient, being there. It's about loving the little person so much you sometimes have to sit down because it's so powerful."

"But maybe some people just don't have that gene," she said.

"Parents are made, not born." He poured cream and added two packets of sugar into his coffee.

She sat down and wrapped her hands around her mug. "I looked through Elliot's desk last night and saw two file folders, one with my name, one with my mom's. I'm too chicken to look in either one."

"You don't have to do anything right away," he said. "But I do think you should look at some point. For closure. Whatever the answer is, if there are answers in those files, you'll finally know the truth."

"Do I want to know? That my father was a man who cheated on his wife for twenty-five years? Who turned my mother and me into the town outcasts? I'm not saying he did that alone—my mother chose to have an affair with a married man, to stay with him and raise me in this town where everyone would judge us. But at least she was there—some of the time. He never was. And if I discover he's not my father? Then I'm the daughter of some unknown weeklong fling with one of three different possibilities? I don't even know their names."

"I'm sorry, Bethany. I know it's hard either way. But better to deal with something and find your peace with it than let it haunt you."

"I'm not haunted."

"No? It's had a huge impact on your life. Maybe knowing the truth could help you let go."

"Maybe," she said. "Or it might just make me feel really, really bad."

He reached over and took her hand. "I'm here for you, okay?"

She squeezed his hand and then let go, taking a bite of the pie, which was delicious.

All too soon, their pie was gone, their mugs drained. She wasn't ready for him to go.

When she walked him and sleeping Wyatt to the door, they both took a piece of her heart with them.

Chapter Seven

"That's it, Danny! Good job!" Shane called, keeping a close eye and ear on how the boy was handling the training skills he'd just gone over with him and Pickles. Danny had been right on time at 3:30 p.m. and their session was winding down.

Danny beamed and knelt beside the scruffy little gray terrier mix. "Good, Pickles!" he said, giving the dog a treat and then a few kisses on the head.

Shane grinned. Danny was a great kid, full of life. He talked a mile a minute, shared his every thought and feeling, and laughed as easily as he teared up. Luckily, there'd been only one tearful moment. Pickles had refused to budge in the middle of the loop when he was supposed to be walking nicely at Danny's side. Shane had assured him that sometimes dogs got tired, or their bellies hurt, or they just got plain stubborn and it was okay to give them a minute. A few seconds later, Pickles responded and they were back on track.

As Danny's mom came through the gate to pick him up, Shane waved and then let her know what a great job Danny and Pickles had both done today. As the three left, the terrier's tail wagging away, Danny telling his mom all about the session, Shane felt a pang. In eight years, Wyatt would be Danny's age. His parents seemed like great people, great parents, but the elementary years had to be hard. The teen years harder.

Shane swallowed, again walloped by a feeling of failure. He could have worked harder at his marriage, tried to be more of what his ex-wife wanted and needed. But now his focus had to be on getting everything right, not letting Wyatt down in other ways. And yet he couldn't stop trying to come up with excuses for going over to Furever Paws to see Bethany. She was becoming too important to him and she'd only been back a couple days.

His phone pinged with a text. His mother.

How's my Princess? You can let her know I'm coming home early—the day after tomorrow. Your aunt is driving me bonkers! I'll be back around 3 pm.

A lead balloon seemed to drop into his stomach. The day after tomorrow was too soon. There was that matter of a certain conversation that would be had. And his excuse for being next door to Bethany's house four times a day would be gone.

His mother hadn't mentioned hearing that Bethany had inherited Elliot's house, but she never brought up Bethany. He used to think it was because she hadn't known they were a serious couple, hadn't realized how much Bethany meant to him. His gut burned at the fact that his mother had known exactly how much she'd meant to him, which was why she'd manipulated Bethany out of his life.

He'd have to have another conversation with his mother about being neighborly if and when she happened to see Bethany coming or going. A wave, a hello.

But his mother was a lot like Princess. Very stubborn.

Shane thought he heard a cry and whirled around, then remembered Wyatt wasn't here. He'd dropped off Wyatt at Grant and Rebekah's for a playdate with the Whitaker twins. And this afternoon, Nina and her boyfriend would pick him up and he wouldn't be back for a few days.

Shane sighed, already missing Wyatt like crazy.

He might only have his son part-time, but he was a full-time father. Fatherhood first. His attraction to

Bethany Robeson would get him nowhere but drop-kicked to the curb like twelve years ago. She was leaving in a few weeks.

He had to remember *that* instead of the way she'd felt in his arms last night.

Twenty-one dogs and one cat were set for pickup by Furever Paws within a half hour.

Twenty-one dogs. There were three currently in the kennels: Meatball, Mikey and one puppy still under veterinary care. Twenty-one would put them at maximum. Things were about to get *very* busy.

"All I have to say is, thank the heavens you're here," Birdie said to Bethany as they left Birdie's office. "If I'd gotten that call from Wendell's Animal Control two days ago, without a full-time director? I'm not sure I could have said yes to taking all those dogs."

All those dogs were the result of a terrible "backyard breeder" crisis in Wendell, a few towns away from Spring Forest. The local sheriff's department closed down the place, the state ASPCA arriving to help with the huge number of dogs on the property. All purebreds, from German shepherds to Labrador retrievers—and all in need of medical care. The ASPCA called shelters and rescues within one hundred miles for help, and everyone who could stepped up.

Bethany, Birdie and two volunteers were getting ready to take the two Furever Paws trucks—outfitted with kennels lined up and ready to be filled—over to Wendell, when Bethany realized she could really use Shane's expertise on this from the get-go. He could do an immediate assessment of temperament and adoptability. Dogs that could go into foster care right away or be adopted quickly would make room for more pooches that needed rescuing.

She texted him about the situation and asked if he was free to lend a hand.

No problem. See you in a few.

Always. Always there when she needed him. She couldn't get used to that.

Couldn't get used to needing him either.

Ten minutes later, Shane arrived with an extra truck and extra kennels, just in case.

"You're a superhero," Birdie called out to him. "Bethany, you ride with Shane, fill him in. I'll take one truck, and the volunteers the other."

Bethany knew what Birdie was doing. Even as she focused on the dogs in crisis, she was also trying to help wherever she could, and that included poking into Bethany's love life.

"Did your sitter return?" Bethany asked as she got into his truck. He closed her door for her, then came around the front and got beside her, smelling delicious. A little soapy, a little citrusy maybe. How he didn't smell like dog was beyond her. But he never did. She was sure *she* did.

"Actually, Wyatt is on a playdate with the Whitaker twins," he said, as he reversed and followed the two Furever Paws trucks down the road. "Lily and Lucas are a month younger, but they're best buds. Grant is on playdate duty—three babies on his own, that's a dad who knows what he's doing."

Bethany smiled. "Rebekah's at Furever Paws. She was actually supposed to leave an hour ago but I overheard her on the phone, letting Grant know he'd have to handle the playdate himself because she wanted to get the staff and kennels ready for the new dogs. I didn't realize the playdate was with Wyatt."

"I'll have to return the favor," he said. "Though I'm pretty used to one baby. Three might send me over the edge."

She smiled. "You seem like you have it completely together. I think you'd handle it just fine."

"Single fatherhood, even half the week, has its rough times, trust me. But I appreciate the vote of confidence," he said, turning onto Main Street, which would lead to the highway out of town. "Hey, how'd it go with Harris this morning? Did he come by?"

The tall, handsome man with light brown eyes

flashed into her mind. "He sure did. He seems like a great guy and really knows his stuff. Everything he said sounded like magic—it doesn't seem possible that he can get so much done at such a reasonable price. And since he'll take a percentage of the selling price, I can afford him. I'll need to stay somewhere else for a few days, though, since he'll be painting and then working on the upstairs bathroom. I'll have to be out of the way."

"You'll stay with me," he said. "Cheaper than renting a room, and I'm a really good cook."

She bit her lip, loving the idea and scared of it at the same time. She had no money for an extended motel stay. *Accept his offer. It's a place to stay; you're not sharing a bedroom.* And hadn't he said it was a big house? "I appreciate that."

She imagined Shane Dupree making her an omelet, pouring her orange juice. While he was fresh out of the shower, his hair damp, just low-slung jeans on his narrow, sexy hips.

That line of thinking was why staying at his place was so risky.

They arrived at the ordinary-looking house in Wendell, and thoughts of Shane half naked *poofed* out of her head. The Furever Paws team hopped out of the trucks and headed around back.

As soon as the ASPCA staffer—a woman who introduced herself as Vanessa—opened the gate to the large fenced yard, Bethany's heart clenched and she shook her head. There were at least sixty dogs and puppies roaming the fenced yard, and she knew that many had already been picked up by other rescues.

These poor beautiful creatures, she thought. How could anyone treat them this way?

Vanessa introduced the team to the ASPCA staff, and handed Bethany a list of the twenty-one dogs she'd be taking. Birdie stood beside her, both of them scanning the paper. The more she read, the more her eyes widened.

> *3 pregnant golden retrievers.*
> *5 younger golden retrievers, 3 boys, 2 girls.*
> *4 male German shepherds.*
> *3 cockapoo puppies, 1 boy, 2 girls.*
> *2 pregnant chocolate Labrador retrievers.*
> *3 young male Labrador retrievers, one yellow, two black.*
> *1 female Labrador retriever, black, and 1 male Siamese who seem to be a bonded pair, believed to have been the backyard breeder's personal pets.*

Bethany looked at Birdie. "That's a lot of pregnant dogs!"

Birdie grimaced. "Which means a lot, and I mean a *lot*, of puppies soon."

"Well, at least puppies are always easy to find homes for," Shane said.

"Let's just hope the mamas aren't too sick," Bethany said, shaking her head.

Most of the dogs were very thin, a few were visibly injured—either limping a bit or bearing obvious scrapes. Others looked ill, even with their wagging tails. Bethany just hoped it wasn't too late for them to be truly saved and restored to health.

The ASPCA had told Bethany over the phone that the owners of the "business" had received citations and had disappeared some time last night, knowing that the sheriff was coming to shut them down.

"Well, let's get our new furry friends back to Furever Paws," Birdie said. "Doc J will round up a couple of his veterinarian friends to come help with the examinations. Once we know what's what, we can get going on foster placements."

Bethany had looked through the updated roster of available fosters—there were a good number, but not twenty-one. This many new animals in need of care and treatment and assessment would create a crisis in both funds and space. But a rescue center had to find a way to be ready for a crisis, and Furever Paws was on it, one way or another.

Once back at the shelter, Birdie put Bethany and Shane on naming duty while she went to talk to Doc J about rounding up his veterinarian posse.

They were in the kennel room, the three current residents moved to private offices for the time being. Meatball and Mikey were now in Bethany's office in their cushy beds with toys and a snack, and the other puppy was in Birdie's office.

Each newly rescued dog was now in a kennel with a bed and a few toys—thanks to donations that had come pouring in once Birdie got the word out about the situation. After each dog was examined, they'd be fed, then groomed, and a plan would be put in place. The beautiful Siamese cat was in a little kennel just outside the cat room—and making a ton of noise. Bethany had given him a catnip toy to play with, but the cat hadn't touched it, just meowed. Poor guy was scared and confused, as the dogs were. But right now, being kept separate until his exam was the best thing for him.

They had only about fifteen minutes to name all twenty-two newcomers. Bethany liked the idea of the dogs getting named before their exams, so everyone could start using a familiar name and making the dogs feel comfortable.

They walked along the row of kennels. The three pregnant golden retrievers were side by side. The beautiful mamas-to-be looked almost identical. "Buttercup, Tulip and Daisy," Bethany said, writing their names on the small white board that hung on each kennel. She looked at the goldens and nodded.

"That was fast," Shane said.

"Sometimes dogs just name themselves," she said with a smile. "You're next. The five other goldens. Three boys, two girls."

Shane knelt down, all five sitting up curiously. "Hmm, let's see. All a bit shy—no surprise, given the crowded and chaotic situation they were just removed from. They seem in okay health. I think this group will move quickly out of here."

"Agreed," she said. "They seem to be around eighteen months or so. I wonder why the backyard breeders didn't sell them."

"Prime moneymakers for more pups," Shane said, shaking his head.

She was disgusted and heartsick at how those people had treated the innocent animals in their care. "Ah, I'm sure you're right. At least these young goldens are in relatively good shape—especially compared to the condition of all the other dogs, ranging from clearly unsocialized and kept in kennels too long to various states of unwell."

A volunteer, who was a student at a nearby university, came in with a tray stacked with twenty-one stainless-steel food bowls.

"You can just leave those and we'll distribute them," Bethany told her. "Thanks so much."

"I'm stuck on names for them," Shane said. He looked at the volunteer. "Want to help me name these gorgeous goldens?"

The college student brightened. "Alpha, Beta, Epsilon, for the guys," she said without missing a beat. "Delta and Gamma for the girls."

Bethany laughed. "They're frat bros and sorority sisters?"

"Definitely," the girl said with a grin before leaving.

Bethany smiled at the five beautiful goldens. "Greek it is, then!"

Birdie came in, peering at the names Bethany had written on the white boards on each kennel. "Can I do the honors of the four way-too-skinny male German shepherds?"

"Sure," Bethany said.

"This one is Jethro," Birdie said. "He's Joshua. That's Jester. And that poor dear," she added, pointing at the very sickly-looking one, "is Jedidiah." She kneeled down in front of his kennel. "Jedidiah, sweetheart, we're going to make you feel better very soon. Don't you worry."

The majestic shepherd lifted his eyes to Birdie, if not his head, which rested on his front paw.

"Cockapoo puppies," Shane said as they walked to the next group of kennels. Inside were the three adorable black-and-white pups, no more than four or five months. They were huddled together, looking nervous. "This little guy is Chaplin. And the two girls are Monroe and Harlow. They're definitely going to need socialization before they're ready for adoption."

In the next two kennels were the two pregnant chocolate Labrador retrievers. "I've got it. Cocoa and…" Bethany tilted her head, staring at the lovely dog. "Godiva!"

"Perfect," Birdie said.

"Oh, these three guys are easy to name," Shane said, moving to the next kennels, each holding a young male Lab. One was yellow and two were black. "The yellow dude is Texas. This one here, Utah. And that gorgeous fellow is Dakota."

Bethany smiled. She loved those names.

And finally there was the female black Lab who looked to be around three years old, who the ASPCA staffer said had been the backyard breeder's pet— along with the Siamese cat. Bethany could tell right away that the dog needed training. She didn't seem aggressive but she was emitting a low growl, letting everyone know that she was in unfamiliar territory and was not happy about it. But at least she seemed healthy.

"Pepper," Bethany said, writing her name on the white board. "And we'll name your former house-mate, the silver Siamese, Salty, since he does seem a bit salty making that racket." Bethany kneeled down and spoke in a gentle voice. "I know you're scared, Pepper. I know this place is unfamiliar. But we're going to treat you very well."

"That's right," Birdie said to the pretty Lab. "And since you were last to be named, you can be first to go see Doc J. Two of his veterinarian buddies will be arriving shortly, and the three will assess all twenty-two newcomers. They're bringing two vet techs too."

"Such a relief," Bethany said.

"They're donating their services for today, but that's just for the exam," Birdie said. "They'll have to charge for any needed treatment. We also need to find the money for extra food and supplies. It's going to put quite a strain on our resources. And that's not even counting the man-hours from the staff and volunteers to handle assessments and figure out who's ready for foster care or immediate adoption."

"I'll get started on a fundraising plan and adoption drive," Bethany said.

"And I'll assess all the dogs for temperament,

training potential, adoptability, on the house," Shane said. "My pleasure."

"I appreciate that, Shane," Bethany said, touching his arm.

His gaze went to her hand, his expression…full of so much she couldn't pin down any one emotion. Flustered, she pulled her hand away.

Birdie gave a firm nod. "I always say that Shane Dupree is a hell of a guy."

"Then why did one of my poodle trainees pee on my boot today at Barkyard Boarding?" Shane asked with a grin.

Bethany couldn't help but laugh. Somewhere in this conversation, between all the names and a peeing poodle, Bethany realized she was falling in love all over again with this kind, generous, gorgeous man. There was no stopping that train—but she reminded herself that she didn't have to act on it. Her plan hadn't changed. As soon as the house was sold and the shelter had a new director, she'd be gone.

But until then, how was she going to stay with him without risking everything she'd worked so hard to achieve the past twelve years? Like the protective brick wall around her heart that kept her safe. How?

Chapter Eight

When dogs were your business, camping out in a sleeping bag on the floor of an animal rescue with barkers, whiners, scratchers and noisy toy chewers was just par for the course. What *wasn't*? Having that sleeping bag three feet away from Bethany's.

It was just past eight o'clock. Bethany hadn't been comfortable leaving the overnight shift for volunteers to handle given the high number of dogs and their varied needs. So when she mentioned she'd be camping out in the dog room, Shane said he would too. After all, he'd been there from the get-go with this crew, had even named some of them, and was already attached.

To the dogs. And to Bethany.

He'd left for a couple hours earlier to pick up Wyatt from his playdate, spend some time with him, and get him ready to spend the next couple of days with his mom, then Shane had returned to Furever Paws. His own staff, two of whom worked the overnight shift at Barkyard Boarding, knew if they had any issues, they could call and he'd be over there in a flash.

So here he was with Bethany Robeson, sharing take-out Chinese food—sesame chicken for her, beef in garlic sauce for him, and pint of vegetable fried rice. They were leaning against the far wall of the room, their containers between them, plates balanced on their laps.

She heaped some sesame chicken onto his plate before he could even ask if he could try some. He reciprocated with the beef, and then they dug in.

Like old times. They'd had Chinese food a few times during their six months together, taking their picnic to the park or into the woods, trying to eat with chopsticks and finally both mastering it about a month into their romance. She'd feed him a bite, he'd feed her a bite, then they'd crack open their fortune cookies and see what they got. Sometimes the fortune was just right. Sometimes it didn't apply at all. Sometimes they'd shake their heads and laugh.

And then they'd kiss and make love, and Shane

would feel like he had everything he'd ever really needed. His family might have been falling apart around him, but when he was with Bethany, his world was okay and all the bad stuff that kept him up nights floated to the edge of his consciousness. Bethany had him. And he had her.

Bethany took a bite of her sesame chicken. "Remember when we'd close our eyes and twirl our fingers around the menu and where it landed was what we ordered? I found out I liked tofu that way. Well, sautéed tofu in an incredible sauce with lots of veggies."

He laughed. "I remember. I remember it all, Bethany."

Jeez. He hadn't meant for his voice to turn so serious, so reverent. But there was very little chance of hiding his real feelings when she was around.

"Me too," she said.

For a few moments they ate in silence.

"Thanks for helping me here," she said. "You've done a lot of that since I've been back."

"Anytime. And I mean that."

"Ditto," she said.

He reached over and squeezed her hand but didn't let go. And suddenly he was looking—with that seriousness, with that reverence—into those green eyes that had also kept him up nights when he couldn't stop thinking about her. They both leaned in at the same time, the kiss soft, tender, then with all the pent-up passion they'd clearly both been feeling these last days.

Everything came rushing back. How much he'd loved her twelve years ago, how he'd barely been able to be away from her, counting the minutes until they could be together. How drawn he still was to her. And how much he wanted to keep kissing her. Despite, despite, despite...

She pulled slightly away. "Uh-oh."

He let out a rough exhale, trying to pull himself together. "Right? You're leaving in a couple weeks. Maybe three tops. And I'm solely focused on being the best father I can be. So that's two really good reasons why we shouldn't kiss again." Except he leaned in again.

And so did she. This time there was nothing soft or tender about the kiss. Instead, it was pure passion. His hand wound in her silky brown hair, her hands on his face.

A puppy started barking, then another, then yet another. The three cockapoos.

"They're saving us from getting into trouble," Bethany said, glancing at the time on her phone. "Time for their potty break. They'll be interrupting us all night, so that should keep us in line."

He smiled. "We can get into a lot of trouble in between, though." Okay, he didn't mean to say that.

"You know Birdie is gonna come by at least twice," Bethany said. "And I'm sure Rebekah will pop by to see how we're doing. Plus we have an audience of twenty-one," she added, popping up and collecting their plates. "It's like we have a bunch of furry chaperones."

Shane reluctantly got up too, picking up the containers and stuffing everything into the big bag it all came in. Shane leashed up two of the pups, and Bethany took the other. They were being fussy, but Shane could hardly blame them. Their first day in the rescue had been exhausting. Brought to a strange place, poked and prodded by the veterinarians, assessed by him and Birdie and Bethany. They must be scared and confused. But tomorrow, most of the dogs would be gone to foster homes, including the puppies, and that would hopefully help them settle down and feel safe.

Bethany and Shane took the cockapoos outside and let them do their business and run around for a while until they were happily tired, then they headed back in. In an hour, they'd bring all the dogs, four at a time into the yard for the last outing of the night, then he and Bethany would keep watch from their spot on the floor in their sleeping bags.

But the thought of those two kisses would keep him awake all night long.

Rebekah had stopped by around ten last night to check on everyone, and Birdie *had* come twice, so it was a good thing the puppies had already stopped them from doing anything foolish and X-rated. Bethany wondered if she would have seen just where that kiss would have led had the cockapoo pups not interrupted. All night, in between a few more trips outside and checking on the dogs who'd been started on medications, Bethany had been very aware of Shane. He'd been so close, as vigilant as she'd been about the dogs, leaping up with concern if he heard the slightest whimper so he could go to reassure a scared pooch.

The sleeping bags had reminded her of their short camping trips, taken just to ensure they'd be alone for a few hours. They'd been so in love back then, so eager for any time they could have together.

Now, the next morning, Bethany glanced at Shane over in the corner of the break room at Furever Paws. She had a pot of coffee going and he was calling Barkyard Boarding to check in. Someone had brought bagels and doughnuts, and she took a half of a cinnamon raisin, dabbed on some butter and gobbled it down. Today would be a busy, long day.

Her phone pinged. It was Leah, the volunteer at the front desk. *The foster is here for Buttercup!*

Bethany consulted her list of fosters that Birdie had arranged yesterday. Lucy Tucker would be taking Buttercup. Seriously, Bethany wished she could afford a bouquet of buttercups or even roses to thank Lucy for offering to foster the very pregnant golden retriever.

"Do you know Lucy Tucker?" she asked Shane, who'd just pocketed his own phone.

"Yup. She's great. She owns the bookstore in town—Chapter One. I think she's been in town for about a year. Nice pet section there, by the way."

"Wonderful," she said. Buttercup was the last of the pregnant goldens still at the shelter.

"We need confetti every time someone comes in to foster or adopt," Shane said.

"Right? I'm so happy!" Birdie and a few staffers had run around the entire county yesterday, doing home checks for new fosters and potential adopters. Lucy Tucker had a star next to her name, which meant she was good to go.

They headed into the lobby. A couple stood by the gift shop area, looking at the dog toys, collars and leashes. With her khaki-hued complexion, wavy dark brown bob and sparkling dark brown eyes, Lucy was absolutely lovely. The man beside her was also

128

very attractive, tall and muscular, with a darker skin tone, light brown eyes and neatly trimmed goatee.

Shane smiled at them. "Lucy Tucker, Calum Ramsey, this is Bethany Robeson, the new temporary director of Furever Paws. Bethany, as I mentioned, Lucy owns Chapter One, the great bookstore in town, and Calum owns Pins and Pints, one of my favorite places to hang out after a long day—a combo bowling alley and bar."

"So nice to meet you," Bethany said. "You two will love Buttercup."

Lucy's eyes widened and Calum coughed.

Oops. She should have known better than to assume that they were a couple just because they were here together. After all, she and Shane were here together and they weren't a couple.

"Just me fostering the golden," Lucy said, extending her hand.

Bethany clasped Lucy's hand with both of hers. "Ah, sorry about that—and thanks so much for helping us out."

Calum smiled. "I'm just being neighborly and helping transport."

"Buttercup will be the new mascot of Chapter One," Lucy said. "I'll be bringing her to work with me."

Bethany grinned. Lucky pooch. "I'll go get her. Our volunteers spent last night putting together ev-

erything each dog would need, so we've got Buttercup all set with a big plush bed, food, bowls, collar
and leash, a blanket and toys, and of course, supplies
for the birth of the pups. And anything else you need,
please just let me know."

Bethany headed into the dog room and knelt in
front of Buttercup's kennel. "Hi there, sweets. You're
going to a wonderful foster home and will get to hang
out at a bookstore." Bethany couldn't help but think
about how many people would meet the beautiful dog
and fill out applications to adopt one of her puppies.

She led Buttercup to the lobby.

"Oh wow," Lucy said, kneeling beside the Golden.
"She's even more beautiful than the photo I saw yes-
terday. Hello, beauty." She gave the dog a warm rub.
"I'm going to foster you and treat you like a queen.
I promise you'll be very comfortable, Mama-to-be."

"You're in excellent hands, Buttercup," Calum
said, his gaze soft on Lucy.

The four got all the dog's new paraphernalia into
Lucy's vehicle, Buttercup in a padded kennel in the
cargo area.

Bethany and Shane waved as the car pulled out
of the gravel lot. "I'm so happy for Buttercup. I *want*
her to be treated like a queen."

"No doubt she will be. And now Calum will have

more excuses to come by the bookstore—to see Buttercup. That man has it bad for Lucy."

"You think so?" Bethany asked.

"I could tell by how he was looking at her."

The way you used to look at me, Bethany thought.

As they headed into the hallway to check on the new crew, Salty the silver Siamese was meowing away. As he had been all last night.

"What's the matter, Salty?" Bethany asked, leaning in front of his kennel. He had food, water, catnip toy, a soft blankie. He was medically cleared for adoption, but because he was meowing so much, Bethany wanted to keep him separated from the other cats for a bit longer.

He also didn't seem to like people—or being handled. *Hey, Salty, hiss away. I get it. I know you'll calm down soon, and we'll see your true personality.*

"I can hear a dog whimpering," Shane said, and they headed into the dog room.

Bethany lifted her head, straining to hear where the whimper was coming from.

"It's Pepper," Shane said. The beautiful female black Lab looked really…glum. Her head was on her paws, and she barely looked up when they knelt down to say hi.

"Oh my goodness," Bethany said. "Of course!"

"Of course what?" Shane asked.

"Pepper looks very sad and is whimpering. Salty has been meowing up a storm since we brought him in. They were the backyard breeder's pets. The ASPCA's notes said they're a bonded pair."

"Ah, now it's my turn to say 'of course.' The separation must be making things doubly hard on them."

"I'll go get Salty. How about if we move Pepper to the very last kennel so she and Salty can share? The dogs are probably accustomed to the scent of Salty since he was on the property, free roaming, but again, everything's new and different for them."

"I'm on it," he said, taking Pepper out of her kennel on her leash and walking her down to the end of the row.

Bethany hurried out and took Salty's cage. The beautiful cat meowed very loudly. "I think you're going to be much happier in five seconds." She took the cage into the dog room, and the dogs barely made a peep. Excellent.

Shane lined up Salty's cage opening with the smaller opening of Pepper's kennel and let the cat inside. Salty ran beside the Lab, licking her furiously on the nose and forehead, then her leg. Pepper gave a giant sigh of contentment and laid back down, tail wagging, Salty curling up in the little space between her chin and chest. The cat's eyes closed. And when a cat closed his eyes, content in his little dog-made cave to nap, all was well in his world.

"Yay," Bethany said. "A real bonded pair. They'll have to be adopted together."

"I know that makes it harder to find a home. And Salty is definitely not a people cat—he's a dog cat. A Pepper-cat, specifically. But maybe he'll warm up to people once he gets used to the staff here. He was likely ignored completely at his old residence."

Bethany smiled at the snoozing cat, the happy dog sheltering her best friend.

"So when should I expect my houseguest?" Shane asked. "Is Harris starting tomorrow morning?"

"Yup. So I guess I'll see you with my bags after work tomorrow? If that's still okay," she added nervously.

They'd kissed last night. Twice. She'd had a really busy morning, but that hadn't stopped her from thinking about the kiss constantly.

"More than okay," he said.

"To be honest, I'm glad to have a reason not to stay at that house. Even if…" She trailed off, not really sure what she'd been about to say. *Even if it puts us in close quarters again. Even if staying at your house makes me feel closer to you when I really can't risk that. Even if we end up ripping each other's clothes off…*

She wouldn't let that happen. Couldn't. Self-preservation. Their lives didn't fit. They were headed down different paths. Bethany to opening her own animal rescue in a town three hours south of Spring Forest. Shane to parenthood. Family.

"You don't have to finish that sentence," he said. "There are a lot of 'even ifs.' Personally I like them all."

So did she.

Chapter Nine

At just past 9:00 p.m., Bethany turned the key in the lock at Elliot's house, looking forward to a hot bath with the lavender-scented bubbles she'd bought yesterday. What a day and night it had been at Furever Paws. Several dogs, the ones cleared for foster homes and even adoption, had left with excited folks, and the staff had conducted many more home checks to clear the way for additional adoptions. The black-and-white cockapoo pups were in high demand as were the young golden retrievers. There'd been several calls asking if Pepper could be adopted on her own, and the answer was a firm no. Pepper was a package deal with Salty.

As she stepped inside the house, Bethany had that same feeling as always. Discomfort. I-don't-belong-here. I-don't-want-to-be-here. After tomorrow, she wouldn't be. Not that she'd be entirely comfortable where she was headed, either. But she'd have the comfort of knowing that this place would look very different in a couple weeks. Harris would have his crew take away all the furniture that couldn't be donated or sold, like the lumpy old recliners. The house would go on the market, hopefully sell quickly, and Bethany would start her new life.

Which meant leaving Spring Forest. Leaving Furever Paws. Leaving that darling Meatball, who she came to love more every day.

And of course, leaving Spring Forest also meant leaving Shane.

Their connection was so intense—in a good way. She could count on him, lean on him, fantasize about him… It might be dangerous to her peace of mind, but it felt so good, she couldn't resist.

Upstairs, she went into the bathroom and drew the bath, pouring in the bubbles, which smelled heavenly. As she lowered herself into the pink tub, it was her turn to sigh in deep contentment. She closed her eyes, Shane's face immediately coming to mind. They'd once taken a bubble bath together when her mother had followed Elliot to a conference in Raleigh.

Her mood soured a bit at the memory of her mom leaving her behind to sneak off with Elliot. But maybe forcing herself to think about her past, her childhood, the rough teenage years, would help clear her head. Or maybe it would just upset her.

Go downstairs and look through the files with your name and your mom's name on them, she told herself.

The bath was cooling anyway, so she wrapped herself in a towel, changed into a long T-shirt and yoga pants, put her hair in a low ponytail and went downstairs. As she passed the recliners in the living room, she had a strange pang in her chest. She didn't know what went on in Elliot and his wife's marriage, but the recliners suddenly seemed like history, memories, a photograph proving there was a marriage, that these two people had lived in this house for decades, had sat in those chairs in whatever kind of agreement they had.

Getting rid of them seemed kind of...disrespectful.

Bethany bit her lip and stared at them. Tonight, she was supposed to go through the house and tape an index card on any of the big pieces of furniture that she didn't want to try to sell. Maybe she should let the recliners stay where they were. Someone might want them, an older couple who might appreciate the broken-in feel. A bit of the history of this house would live on.

That settled, she went into Elliot's office and sat down at the desk. She opened the side drawer and grabbed the folder with her mother's name. She'd just take a look, see what was in there. Probably just letters and photographs.

She put the folder on the desk, sucked in a breath and opened the folder. Empty. That was strange. She reached for the one with her name and pulled it out— flat as the ole pancake. Also empty.

She went through the drawers and folders, expecting to find something had been misfiled. But there was nothing. Had he gotten rid of the evidence of the affair? Any truth about whether he was her father? Or maybe there was nothing to hide because he truly wasn't her father. Maybe he really had left her the house because she was Kate Robeson's child, no other reason. He'd loved Kate, obviously.

Except the lawyer had said that Elliot had "claimed" her as his daughter. What had he meant by that?

Now that she'd had some days to let all this settle— the inheritance, being back in Spring Forest—she'd call or email the lawyer in the morning and ask for clarification.

She got up from the desk and went to the closet. Also empty.

If she was his daughter, she was pretty sure she'd find documentation to that effect in this house. A safe hidden behind a painting or behind a trapdoor in a bureau. If the lawyer had the truth, he likely would have given it to her with the deed paperwork. But there'd been nothing about Elliot being her father. Or not.

She let out a sigh, wishing she had Meatball beside her, his soft yet bristly hair to run her hands through.

But no, what she really wanted was to be in Shane Dupree's arms.

She left the office and forced herself to go through the master bedroom for any documentation. Not a thing.

She was almost relieved. But the room felt like it was closing in on her and she hurried out, closing the door behind her. She went into the guest room to pack her things, feeling the need to get out of there. She wouldn't go to Shane's, not till tomorrow. She was already relying on him too much. Instead, she'd stay at Furever Paws. She'd curl up best she could fit on the love seat in her office. She wanted to be close by if the four sickly German shepherds needed her; they and Pepper and Salty were the only animals left from yesterday's rescue in the dog room. Meatball and his droopy eyes and ears would be a huge comfort, as would sweet Mikey, who was already filling out nicely. She had to admit it would be nice if Meatball and Mikey could talk, help her work through her big questions. Wrap a paw around her shoulders and assure her everything would be all right, that yes, she was dealing with some hard stuff, but she'd come through it fine, and probably more at peace. Like Shane would do and say.

If only she weren't so damned scared of letting herself go, of losing her tight control, letting down her constant guard, she could be in his arms, feeling less alone in the world.

Up to you, Bethany, she reminded herself. She used to think the walls she'd erected around herself meant she was taking care of herself. But lately she wasn't sure.

An hour ago, at just before 11:00 p.m., Shane had come to relieve Birdie and the volunteer on overnight duty at Furever Paws. They hadn't been expecting him, but Shane had texted Birdie with the offer, and the two women were so tired, they'd taken him up on it. He'd be the only one on duty and that was fine.

There weren't that many dogs left, no puppies who'd need multiple potty breaks. He'd sleep, then in the morning he'd check on Princess, head over to Barkyard for the day, and then Bethany would come over.

Bethany—staying with him. And they'd be alone tomorrow night, since he wasn't scheduled to pick up Wyatt until the morning after.

He missed his son terribly. Being in the big empty house without him was hard. Shane constantly heard little sounds, quiet cries, Wyatt's favorite *Ba!*, the mobile playing lullabies. All in his head, of course. The house was dead quiet, and Shane didn't like it.

Shane checked on the German shepherds in the kennel, taking those out whose chart noted they needed an overnight pee break. He went to Pepper and Salty's kennel, noting that Pepper was stretched out, the cat curled up on the inside of Pepper's belly, his pretty silver head on her paw. All was well in their universe.

Bethany had mentioned she'd keep Meatball and Mikey in her office until the shepherds were in better health, so next he checked on those two. They sprang up from their beds with wagging tails, so he took them out into the yard, the two dogs sniffing the spring grass, enjoying the weather even at this late hour. He sat on the step and watched them roam around, then finally headed back inside, putting the dogs back in Bethany's office. Meatball seemed to want to get up on the love seat, but he didn't have the jump in him.

"Soon, Meatball. You'll be in great shape and you'll be able to curl up on the love seat." Mikey probably wanted to make himself comfortable on the plush little sofa but the nice furry guy seemed to know his friend couldn't, so he went to curl up in his bed instead. Meatball got into his bed beside his.

There was a cot in a vacant office beside Doc J's clinic that volunteers on the overnight shift used, a monitor on the table so he could hear anything going on in the dog room. He'd stretch out there. He gave each dog a final pat, shut the door, and then went to his bunk for the night. He'd stuffed a backpack with a light blanket and a change of clothes. He spread the blanket on the cot, took off his boots and socks and laid down, Bethany's face coming right to mind.

When he heard a noise coming from the front, he sat up. A door closed, so someone had definitely come inside the building.

As he opened the door that led into the lobby, he almost crashed right into Bethany.

Her mouth dropped open. "I had no idea you were here."

"Thought I'd give Birdie and the volunteer a break. You were here till nine, I heard. I've got this, Bethany. You should rest up."

"I don't think I can rest in that house," she said. "Too many unknowns. I thought I'd come here where I could be helpful, with some furry company just in case the shepherds need me. I just look at Meatball and feel better."

"I just took him and Mikey out. And the other dogs are in the kennels."

"Furever Paws is really lucky to have you, Shane," she said almost on a whisper, staring at him. Right into his eyes. Down to his lips. Her gaze ran down his neck, across his shoulders, taking in the T-shirt he wore, drifting down to the low-slung sweatpants. His bare feet.

"And you," he whispered back, letting his own gaze do some traveling. How she filled out her sweater, the curves of her leggings. Back up to those green eyes. The beautiful face. *His Bethany.*

He wasn't sure who stepped forward first. Maybe they both did simultaneously. But suddenly they were kissing like it had been twelve years of missing this, needing this, wanting this.

It had been.

He backed her against the wall, his hands sliding into her hair, then under her sweater, his mouth crushed against hers. He couldn't get enough of her, the feel of her in her arms, pressed to him, her perfume driving him wild. She took his hand and pulled him into the vacant office with the cot and closed the door, twisting the lock on the knob.

The light was off, but enough moonlight filtered through the paper window shade to reveal the desire in her eyes as she lifted her sweater, slowly, to give him the opportunity to stop this. He didn't—and she let the sweater drop to the floor.

Oh yeah.

She walked him over to the cot and pushed him down, straddling him while pulling off his Henley shirt, then backing up a bit to get rid of his belt and unfasten his jeans. His heartbeat thundered in his ears. She stood up, sliding down his jeans, and he was glad he wore the black boxer briefs and not the boring plaid boxers. He kicked off his jeans and then freed her sexy lower half of the leggings.

He took in the white lace bra and matching underwear, tiny nothings he could rip off her body with one yank. But he wanted to savor this. Twelve years was a long time to wait for the only woman who'd ever had him enthralled.

He lay down on top of his blanket and gently pulled her onto him, their underwear all that separated them. His hands roamed inside the bra until he had to see her. He unclasped it and she arched her back, the exposure of her full, high breasts making him even harder than he was a second ago. He leaned up and let his hands and mouth explore each one, her breathy moans having a field day with his self-control.

And then she reached inside the boxer briefs, and he had to hold himself very still for a moment, which elicited a giggle in his ear along with a lick. He closed his eyes, aware of his underwear being slid down his legs until he kicked them off.

"I've had the same condom in my wallet for the past three years," she said.

He smiled. "I have a newer one." He grabbed his jeans and fished his wallet out, finding the condom he kept there just in case, even if he hadn't been interested in using it since his divorce.

Don't let yourself think, he told himself. *Just* feel.

He kept his eyes on Bethany as she wriggled out of her own underwear and straddled him again, and then Shane couldn't think if he wanted to.

I never want this to end was his last conscious thought before they exploded together, their hands clasped above their heads, their mouths one, their hearts beating the same thunder.

Bethany awoke with a start, no idea where she was until she realized her head was resting against Shane's upper arm. He was asleep and facing her, the early morning casting shadows on his gorgeous face. They were on the cot in the vacant office. From the hazy light, it was just about sunrise, probably around 6:30. Her phone confirmed it was 6:23 a.m.

She smiled at the thought of how she'd walked into Furever Paws, had a two-second conversation with Shane, and suddenly they were naked and unable to get enough of each other.

She did feel good. Very good. Her shoulders weren't tight. Her mind was clear. Her heart felt... full. Everything she'd needed she'd gotten with Shane last tonight.

But it wasn't about sex or release of all the pent-up frustrations from every aspect of her life. Sex with another man would have also felt good, but the aftermath would have been lonely.

She felt anything but lonely right now.

A little nervous, yes. But for the first time in a long time, she felt like everything was okay.

So why was she inching away from the warmth of his well-built body? Why was she reaching for her yoga pants and T-shirt as if she couldn't escape fast enough?

"Oh no, you don't," came the sexy, sleepy voice of the guy beside her. He wrapped a strong arm around her, pulling her back close, kissing her neck.

"Shane, the first staffers will arrive at seven," she said. "We've got to get ourselves decent."

"I like us like this," he whispered, trailing kisses along her collarbone.

She closed her eyes and tried to let herself just feel, to enjoy the moment, but something about the light of day, people coming and the busy hours ahead crowded her mind.

Excuses, likely. She was just plain scared of what she felt for Shane, and the intimacy between them right now was so real, so raw that she couldn't handle it.

She wriggled away and quickly dressed.

"Darn," he said. "I miss you already."

That got a smile out of her, but anxiety quickly made it drop away. "Shane, I don't know about this. Any of it. And since I'm going to be staying with you…"

She was right. They didn't know what they were doing and they should. He had more to think about than just himself now.

He nodded, but what he would give to have her back in his arms for even a moment.

"I'm not really an 'act first, think later or never' kind of person," she said.

"Me either. But both of us were spontaneous last night—and I think it went pretty well, don't you? So maybe we should just accept it was what we needed."

She bit her lip. "I'm going to dash into the restroom."

"I'll see you tonight, Bethany Robeson," he said, sitting up and sliding the dark blue Henley over his glorious, muscled chest. For a moment, she just had to stare and appreciate his body. His face.

"See you tonight," she managed to croak out, and then fled the room.

Chapter Ten

The next hours were so busy that Bethany barely had time to think about Shane. About last night. Every amazing moment of it. Or how unsettling the unknown of it all was.

We don't have to know what we're doing, he'd said.

But he knew that she always needed to know what she was doing, where she stood. Maybe that was rooted in an insecure childhood. Regardless, it was how she lived her life now. Nothing up in the air. Course set. Plans made.

So many people came in to fill out adoption forms that worrying about staying at Shane's for a couple weeks couldn't even take center stage in her mind.

There were already close to a hundred applications for the puppies that would be born in coming weeks, Goldens and Labs.

No one had expressed interest in the four too-thin male German shepherds who were all undergoing varying degrees of medical treatment, even though the four would be fine—eventually.

Folks wanted cute and young and healthy. Bethany understood. People were busy with jobs and families, and pets were about enhancing their lives. In order to responsibly adopt a pet that needed care or constant vigilance, you had to have the time and the temperament. That wasn't everyone and that was okay. The most important thing in a dog finding his forever home was the match. The right fit.

The sweet family who'd expressed interest in adopting Mikey had come in this morning, the twin boys so in love with him that they couldn't stop smiling. A staffer would be conducting a home check today, and if all was well, Mikey could be going to his forever home by tonight. She'd miss him, and she knew Shane would too.

As would Meatball. Bethany sat in her office on the love seat, the basset hound at her feet, his head on her left foot, slowly causing it to fall asleep. But she had to get up anyway—sorry, sweet Meatball— because the front desk just texted her to let her know her 2:00 p.m. was here.

She headed into the lobby, where a pretty woman in her early thirties stood looking at the artwork of the dogs and cats on the walls. Her shoulder-length dark hair was in a pretty French braid.

"Wendy Alvarez?" Bethany said, extending her hand. "I'm Bethany Robeson, interim director of Furever Paws."

The woman turned, her light green eyes warm and friendly. Wendy shook her hand. "I'd love to meet the dogs Furever Paws rescued yesterday and see if any might be right for our Pets for Vets program. I'm a volunteer, and we train dogs to support veterans emotionally, physically, mentally."

"The program is absolutely wonderful—and vital," Bethany said. "Right this way." She headed toward the door that led to the kennels. "Many of our dogs from the rescue are already in foster homes or on the verge of being adopted, but we have four German shepherds here at the shelter who are on the road to recovery."

The shepherds immediately perked up when they came in.

Wendy smiled. "I love German shepherds. They're among the smartest of dog breeds. Very trainable, especially for a program like Pets for Vets."

"Our veterinarian said they'll all be cleared medically, but he couldn't give a solid time frame since they have different treatment plans. Can you still get a sense of their suitability for the program?"

"I think so," Wendy said. "Is it all right to take them into the yard so we have some room?"

Bethany and a volunteer leashed up the shepherds, and they all headed out. Off leash, the dogs roamed and sniffed, enjoying the early spring sunshine and the low sixties temperature.

Wendy sat down very suddenly on the grass, hanging her head.

"Are you all right?" Bethany asked.

"I am," Wendy said with a nod. "Just doing a little testing, actually."

Jedidiah, the most ill of the shepherds, immediately came over to Wendy. He sat by her side and licked her hand. Then he very gently nudged the side of her head with his snout.

"Good boy!" Wendy said, popping up. "This dog has definitely had some prior training. When I 'lost my balance' and needed to sit down fast, he responded right away. And did you see how he nudged me with his nose? He can tell I have a headache. I took some pain reliever right before I came in, but he was definitely able to sense it. That kind of training takes at least six months, so I'm sure that someone has worked with this shepherd in the past."

"Wow!" Bethany said, petting Jedidiah, and then Jethro, who ambled over to sniff Wendy's shoes.

Jester and Joshua padded over too, wagging their fluffy tails. "Dogs are amazing."

"They absolutely are. I'd love to come back and do a formal assessment in a few weeks when they're healthier. The ones that pass the testing I'd then take up north for further training. I work with an ex-army pilot in the Pilots for Paws program who helps with transport."

"So many wonderful programs and dedicated volunteers," Bethany said. She looked at Jedidiah— skinny, unwell, but on the mend and already trained with valuable skills that could help others. "I wonder how a dog with training, all these beautiful shepherds, ended up at that awful backyard breeder."

"I'm just glad they're all safe now," Wendy said. She handed Bethany her card, gave each of the German shepherds a hearty pat and then left.

"Aww, you guys might all be part of the Pets for Vets program," Bethany said as she and the volunteer led the dogs back into the kennels. "How wonderful would that be?"

Once back in her office, she leashed up Meatball, put on his Adopt Me banner and headed out for his half-mile walk. If someone were interested in adopting him, Bethany would make sure that person would commit to getting Meatball in shape. For now, the basset hound would start slow and they'd work up to covering a full mile over the course of a day. Basset hounds were low to the ground with short legs and couldn't walk too far in one outing. "Slow and steady, am I right, Meatball?"

As they walked along Main Street, many folks smiled at the sweet dog. Meatball turned to look up at her, and her heart melted to the point that she had to stop walking. She knelt beside him and gave him a kiss on the head and stroked his droopy ear. "You're just the best, Meatball." She loved all the dogs at Furever Paws, but Meatball was special.

He resumed walking, his tail wagging. A family headed her way asked if they could pet him, and the dog was so gentle that of course they could. Meatball got tons of love on his walk. She let everyone who stopped to pet him know that he was available for foster or adoption, but after hearing his age and seeing his girth and slow plod, there were just non-committal smiles and nods. Which she also understood. She'd rather he went to someone who had the time and dedication to getting him healthy.

A couple of hours later, Bethany finally clicked off her laptop in her office, her fundraising ideas and outreach plan ready for Birdie's approval. After walking through the shelter, checking in with staff and the volunteers taking the overnight shift, it was close to seven and she was able to leave. There was always work to be done at a rescue, whether going over the budget, checking inventory, approving staff schedules, walking the dogs, playing with the cats, stacking the washed bowls, or folding a load of blankies, but nervous as she was about staying with Shane for a while, she couldn't wait to see him.

She wasn't sure how long she'd be living with him. Harris said she should plan on being out of the house for two weeks. Two weeks. If things got… complicated, she could always dip into her meager savings and find a place to stay in town. Or move into her office temporarily.

Her phone pinged: Got called into Barkyard for a possible emergency. Front door is open, head on in and make yourself comfortable. I shouldn't be long. -S

She had this vision of sitting at his kitchen table with a cup of herbal tea and a slice of pie, Shane coming through the door as though he were her husband. As though she were his wife.

She'd had a lot of those fantasies during their brief romance about "one day," but letting herself get carried away was dangerous. They weren't headed for marriage. Their lives were just too divergent, their needs too different.

She was walking out the front door of Furever Paws when a blond woman in her early forties approached, pulling a child's red wagon containing a huge bag of dog food. Yes! Another food donation. Just what they needed right now.

"Hi, I'm Bethany Robeson, interim director of Furever Paws."

"Josie Whitaker," the woman said, "with a delivery I'm sure you could use. I brought a pie over to a sick neighbor and he said, 'Hey, aren't you related to the Whitakers who run the animal shelter? My three Great Danes refuse to eat their new food and I stupidly bought two huge bags, so you can have the unopened one.' It's fifty pounds!"

"I really appreciate that," Bethany said. "Oh wait—Rebekah mentioned that her sister-in-law had moved into their garage apartment to help with the twins."

"That's me," Josie said. "Grant's sister. I love those little munchkins."

Bethany grinned. "They were guest stars at our staff meeting on my first day. They're adorable."

"You look like you're heading out. No need to worry about showing me where to go—I've brought in donations before," Josie assured her. "But I'm glad I got the chance to meet you. I'm sure I'll be seeing you around here. I do a lot of stress cooking and tend to share my creations."

Bethany smiled, sensing there was a lot behind that last part. She liked Josie immediately. "I stress *eat*, so we're a pair for sure."

Josie grinned and Bethany held open the door so Josie could wheel in the wagon.

Okay. Time to go to Shane's. For two weeks… Oh, yes, she'd be stress eating, all right.

When she arrived, an SUV that she didn't recognize was parked in the driveway. His personal vehicle, she assumed, since he'd probably taken his work truck to Barkyard Boarding.

Bethany slung her tote bag over her shoulder and got out her suitcase, then headed to the front door. She felt a bit weird about just opening the door and walking in, but that was what Shane had said to do.

As she went up the steps, she heard barking. Familiar barking. It was Princess. She opened the door to find the little Chihuahua barking away at her.

"Aw, don't you remember me, Princess?" she cooed. "It's Bethany. Did Shane leave you all alone while he had to go to work for a bit? No worries, sweetie. I'm going to be staying here for a while. I'll keep you company."

Bethany could swear she heard a gasp—a human gasp. Then footsteps. Coming from the kitchen.

And then standing there in the hallway, and scowling at her, was Anna Dupree.

Shane's mother.

As Shane turned the corner onto his street, he did a double take as he looked up ahead into his driveway. Two cars. One was Bethany's.

The other, his mother's.

She wasn't due back in Spring Forest till *tomorrow.* Oh damn.

He sped up and parked, noticing Bethany through the open front door. She stood inside with her bags. He could see his mother, hands on hips, just beyond Bethany.

He raced up the steps. "Mom, you're a day early." He shot a look of commiseration to Bethany, who looked like the ole deer caught in headlights.

"Is that a crime?" his mother asked, walking over, around Bethany without looking at her, to give him a peck on the cheek. Princess sat beside her, staring at him. Like: *Try to tell me what to do now, trainerman!* "I stopped over to leave you a key lime pie for taking care of my baby girl."

"Just didn't expect you," he said.

She lifted her head, smoothing her chin-length ash-blond hair. "Obviously. Since you didn't mention you were now shacking up with someone." She turned to Bethany, looking her up and down. "Elliot's house wasn't enough for you, huh?"

He saw Bethany flinch, though she didn't say anything. She looked too stunned to respond, not that his mother deserved a response.

"Mom, I'm going to make myself very clear," Shane said. "Do *not* speak about or to Bethany disrespectfully. This is *my* house."

Bethany's eyes widened, and he could see a vein working on her neck.

"Oh, is that how it is?" his mother said in a wounded tone. "I'll be leaving then!" With that, she picked up Princess and marched out.

Shane shut the door, a hot burst of anger pulsating inside him. "I'm very sorry you got ambushed like that. I knew she was coming home early, but she was supposed to arrive tomorrow. Not tonight."

"Guess she still hates me," Bethany said. "Another reason why…" She trailed off, shaking her head.

He stared at her. "Why what? Why this won't work? Why we shouldn't even try for a second chance?"

"Yes, exactly," she said. She hoisted up her bags and turned toward the door.

No. Absolutely not. "Bethany, don't give her that power. You're here because you need a place to stay. You're here because I want you here. And hopefully because you want to be here. So let me show you the guest room." He jogged to the stairs, hoping she'd follow.

She took in a breath and then did.

Chapter Eleven

The guest room was very nice. Comfortable bed, fluffy rug, a big framed map of North Carolina. Blackout shades on the windows. None of that helped Bethany forget what had just happened with his mother, though.

She and Shane were now in his living room, on opposite ends of the plush tan sofa, Bethany's legs curled under her. Shane had made them each a margarita, and had set down a basket of tortilla chips with very good salsa beside it. Both of them had grimaced at the sight of the key lime pie, so they definitely wouldn't be having that reminder for dessert.

The sofa faced a huge stone fireplace, and on the mantel were many photos of Wyatt, some of the baby alone, some with father and son. There was one photo of grandma, father and son. Bethany stared at it.

"So your mother didn't like me. Did she like your ex-wife?" she asked, turning back to Shane.

Shane shook his head. "Not one bit. She didn't like that the pregnancy came before the engagement."

"Did they get along?" Bethany asked.

"Not really," he said. "Nina quickly got tired of trying to win her approval and stopped inviting her over, stopped calling altogether. That didn't sit well either." He shook his head. "They're cordial and polite to each other now. I'll talk to my mother tomorrow and make it clear I'm serious about those boundaries, especially because you might run into her as you check out the progress at Elliot's." He took a sip of his drink. "I need to stop calling it that. It's *your* house."

"Did I tell you I finally went through his files and the ones with my name and my mother's were empty? Even if I *wanted* to find some proof of my paternity, I wouldn't be able to."

"I wonder what he did with all that stuff or why he'd get rid of it when he knew he was leaving you the house. You'd think he'd want to explain himself to you."

She shrugged. "I meant to call the lawyer to see if he had any more info, but today got so busy at Furever Paws I didn't have a chance."

He popped a salsa-laden tortilla chip in his mouth. "Speaking of Furever Paws, if you'd like to foster Meatball here, it's fine with me. I'll erect a temporary fence on the side of the house just for him so he's completely separated from my training yard. Meatball is so gentle that he certainly won't rile up any of my furry clients. You can bring him to work with you every day, then back here."

Bethany bit her lip. She was already way too attached to Meatball for her own good. But having the basset hound come home every night to a big house, a yard of his own and a big comfortable bed to curl up in—meaning the guest room bed—how could she not?

Besides, she was just fostering him. It wasn't like she was adopting him. But having him in a home situation every night was ideal, and would help her efforts to get him healthy and break him out of his shy shell. A wonderful dog lover would definitely fall in love with him then.

"I'd appreciate that, Shane. I'll bring him back here tomorrow night."

Shane's phone pinged with a text, which he read.

"From my mother. 'I told Princess to stay and she actually did. So thank you for that, at least.'"

"Is that her way of trying to make up with you?" Bethany asked. "*At least* aside," she added with a smile.

He leaned his head back for a moment. "Why can't I have a sitcom mom? Words of wisdom, always kind."

"I used to wish I had one too."

"Your mother was always very warm and friendly to me when I saw her," Shane said. "I know she had her issues as a parent, but she was always nice."

Bethany thought about that. It was true. Kate Robeson had been a nice person. She always spoke kindly to Bethany, always kissed her good-night, even when she came home at 2:00 a.m., always told her she was beautiful, including when she had the chicken pox. Her mother truly hadn't thought she'd been doing anything wrong by leaving her five-year-old daughter with sitters for half the night or telling seven-year-old Bethany to make herself a peanut butter and jelly sandwich for dinner—for the third straight night in a row. She'd believed that encouraging fourteen-year-old Bethany to flirt with boys would be helpful. *Every boy will go nuts over you*, Kate would say with a smile. *One will do your homework, another will treat you to pizza and burgers.*

Bethany had never been interested in testing that theory.

Shane's mother on the other hand? Not particularly nice. But always there with nutritionally balanced dinners every night. She'd been the PTA vice president.

Shane pressed a button on his phone, then another and put it down. "I sent her back a dog emoticon."

"You're a good son. Now she won't be tossing and turning all night."

He gulped down the rest of his margarita. "I have a client who's a therapist. I once asked him how to handle a difficult mother who you loved but who drove you nuts."

Bethany leaned forward. "What was his advice?"

"He said, 'You have one mother. If she's not going to change, and she probably isn't, you have to set boundaries that will allow you to have a relationship with her. You have to set limits.'" He swiped another chip in salsa. "So that's what I did. My mom isn't supposed to drop by unannounced, for example, but she clearly did, since she was in the house when you walked in."

"She probably figured you were gone because your truck wasn't there, that she'd drop off the pie and hurry out. Wait—am I defending her?"

Shane smiled. He was about to say something,

but his phone pinged again. "Sorry. Another text. This one from Grant Whitaker. He wants to know if Wyatt and the twins can have a playdate with me tomorrow night. He writes, 'And by playdate I mean free babysitting.'"

It wouldn't be his night to have Wyatt, but he and Nina were always very flexible if a class or play-date came up. Wyatt's needs and happiness always came first with both of them. Being amiably divorced made life *a lot* easier.

Bethany laughed. "Well, I'll be here to help. Not that I know what I'm doing with one baby, let alone three."

"You've got two hands, which means we'll have four total, so that's a major improvement over just mine. If one baby crawls that way, one that way, and one that way," he added, pointing with his crossed forearms, "we'll just have to be superfast to scoop them all up."

Bethany sipped her margarita, suddenly envision-ing herself on the living room floor, babies around her. She certainly wouldn't have seen *that* coming. "I remember you saying you wanted five kids. Do you still?"

"Are you asking so if I say yes, you can worry less about us having that second chance?"

She was surprised at how direct he was, but maybe

it was better to force them to acknowledge what was going on between them. They'd slept together last night. And they hadn't talked about it tonight.

So be direct back, she told herself. *Just say how you feel*.

"To be honest, Shane, sometimes, when I get out of my head, I fantasize about being married. Having *a* child. Along with three dogs and three cats. But then I snap back to reality real fast. You mentioned boundaries and limits. I know mine. They're set for a reason."

He stared at her for a moment. "I loved last night. That's what I know. No boundaries, no limits during every mind-blowing second of it."

She smiled. "I know what you mean. We both really let go. But I think we need to give each other some space here, Shane. There's a lot going on right now. *A lot*."

"I know. For one, I made a promise to myself and my son that I'd focus on being a great father," he said. "That means not getting distracted by a woman who has the power to gut me."

She winced at the phrase *gut me*. But that was how it had felt back then for her, too, so she shouldn't be surprised.

"And then there's the matter of my leaving in two-ish weeks," she said. "And that you did make your promise to yourself and Wyatt. The woman you should fall for should be mother-of-the-year material, not scared to death of the idea of parenthood."

"Bethany," he began, "you sell yourself short."

"Or maybe it's that I know myself."

"Those are boundaries and limits you set for yourself a long time ago, based on a person you're not anymore," he countered. "A teenager. Alone. Hurting."

She lifted her chin. "Well, we can't forget the very current obstacle to anything happening between us, Shane. Your mother despises me."

"There's nothing to hate about you, Bethany Robeson. So whatever my mother's issue is, it's not about you. And trust me, my mother is not an obstacle to us doing whatever we choose. I'm a grown man."

She inwardly sighed. Fine, but she wasn't signing up to deal with the mother from hell. Even if the man involved was heaven-sent.

For so many reasons, she couldn't let herself love Shane Dupree again. She *couldn't.*

So she stood up and told him she was exhausted from the long day and had to be at the shelter an hour early since two volunteers couldn't make it tomorrow for the breakfast round—which was true.

He stood too. He didn't try to stop her. He just took her hand and held it for a moment, then let go.

Walking up the stairs away from him was a lot harder than she expected.

The early morning sun filtered through the curtains, and Shane peeled open one eye and glanced at his phone on his bedside table: 5:58. His alarm would go off in two minutes. He had the 7:00 training class in the backyard this morning.

And someone to make breakfast for. No sprinkle of Cheerios on the high chair, no strained peaches or tiny bits of scrambled egg for a seven-month-old. Wyatt was at Nina's, his sweet face bursting into Shane's mind. *I love you, buddy*, he sent silently in the air. *I miss you like crazy. But I'll pick you up later, and you'll have a fun playdate with your buddies.*

This morning, he would show Bethany how nice it was to wake up in a home with someone else. Just him, nothing too scary like a man and a baby. Slow start. Of course tonight she'd be hit with *a lot* of babies. But babies were fun and funny.

Yes. He could work on changing her mind, her belief system, really, to help her to see that being part of a pack was good, that being a lone wolf was… lonely. He had about two weeks, which was a decent chunk of time. Made a little easier because she'd be right here under his roof.

He remembered how nervous he'd been when Nina was pregnant, that he wouldn't be a good father, that he hadn't had a role model. Everything he once thought he knew about his dad had proven to be a lie when his father had just walked out on his mother and Shane and never looked back. He'd been doubly blindsided—by his father's actions shortly after Bethany dumped him and left. But now he had no choice but to expect the best from himself as a parent—because Wyatt deserved that. Wyatt needed him.

Maybe with someone—two someones—to strive for, Bethany's entire mindset would shift.

Or maybe he was giving himself and his very cute baby son too much credit. He didn't think so, though. There was something beyond special between him and Bethany. You didn't find that kind of connection, chemistry and feeling every day.

They'd come back to each other for a reason. For that second chance. How could he not believe in *that*?

Shane had spent a good part of the night tossing and turning, knowing she was right next door in the guest room, her silky brown hair splayed out on the pillow. He kept trying to come up with excuses to knock on her door. Is your bed comfortable enough?

Do you need an extra blanket? Did I mention that fresh towels are in the closet in the hall?

Or he could have said what he was really thinking: *I can't stop thinking of you. Lying in bed, so close and yet a million miles away. I want to hit repeat on our night in the vacant room at the shelter... every night.*

He had to tread carefully, though. He wasn't even sure they *could* have a second shot together. He *was* focused on Wyatt. Wyatt and Barkyard Boarding—they were his life.

So what then? You're gonna show Bethany how great it is to be part of a family and then send her on her merry way to be with someone else? If you're going to do this, do it.

Admit you want a second chance with Bethany. And commit to it.

He did want it. Bad.

Then you've got a plan. Show her how great this can be. With the right two people—*three* people, including a pint-size one—anything was possible.

He got out of bed and took a hot shower, imagining Bethany with him, all naked and sudsy. As he got dressed, he pictured them sharing a bedroom, a closet, living together, pulling on his T-shirt while she clasped her bra. Brushing their teeth together at their dual sinks. Kissing their way downstairs where they'd take turns making breakfast. Bethany holding Wyatt while he buttered their toast, Shane burping Wyatt while Bethany refilled their coffee.

Togetherness. Family. He had no idea if this fantasy of his was even possible, but regardless, blasting through the wall she'd erected around herself *was*. A happier Bethany would make him happy. Even if he ended up with his heart handed back to him all over again.

When he stepped out of his bedroom, ready to make her an amazing breakfast as part of his plan, he stopped to listen for sounds that she was awake. He heard the shower in the guest bathroom running.

Perfect.

He went downstairs and into the kitchen, getting out the eggs and bacon and English muffins. Back in high school, they'd gone to the diner a few times on Saturday mornings, and she always ordered eggs over easy, crispy bacon and an English muffin.

He got the bacon going, poured some orange juice, made a pot of coffee, and just as the bacon was about ready, he heard footsteps on the stairs.

"I smell something amazing," Bethany called out. She appeared in the doorway, sniffing the air. "Yum."

"Just about to make your eggs. Over easy?"

"Still my favorite," she said. "And you like yours scrambled."

"Me and Wyatt both." He smiled and cracked the eggs in the pan, then dropped the English muffin halves in the toaster.

"Help yourself to coffee or juice," he said. "Breakfast will be ready in a minute."

"You didn't have to do all this." She grinned. "But I appreciate it. I love a home-cooked breakfast that I don't have to make." She passed close by him to pour two mugs of coffee. He could smell her shampoo—the same one he used, the very same one he'd stocked in the guest bathroom—as she moved back to the table. "How about if I make dinner tonight?" she offered.

Cooking in his kitchen for the two of them as he played with Wyatt in the living room? Very homey, very domestic. It fit perfectly into his grand plan.

"That sounds great," he said, sliding her eggs onto a plate and adding the bacon and English muffin.

She smiled at him, then at her plate. "I could get too used to this."

Shane grinned back, taking a sip of his coffee. *That's the idea.*

Chapter Twelve

Bethany was at her desk fine-tuning the fundraising ideas for Furever Paws when her desk phone intercom buzzed. The front desk volunteer told her that someone was here about adopting Salty, the beautiful but standoffish—with people—Siamese cat. The staffer had told the woman that Salty was part of a bonded pair and would only be adopted with Pepper, the black Labrador retriever, but the woman insisted on speaking with a manager.

Some folks would not accept the disappointing news that they couldn't be considered for a particular pet and demanded on speaking to a "higher-up."

Bethany got up with a sigh. She was on a roll with her fundraising brainstorming, particularly after a very productive brainstorming session with Birdie, Rebekah and two staffers on the fundraising committee, but she could use a cup of coffee and a stretch of her legs. She'd had a mug of Shane's great coffee at his house just a couple of hours ago, but she had so much on her mind that she could use another caffeine jolt to help her concentrate.

First, there was Shane and the *too* cozy breakfast they'd shared this morning. The fact that he was going to talk to his mother about last night. And her call to Elliot Bradley's lawyer this morning. He'd reiterated that he had no concrete information about whether or not she was Elliot's biological child. Elliot had told the man only that "I claim Bethany Robeson as my daughter." The lawyer said that sentence had no "legal authority," that people could claim anything without it being verifiably true. There was no documentation in the file, no letter, no anything.

Bethany had gotten a slight headache after that call.

Coffee. She did need coffee. Especially since she was about to deal with someone who insisted on "speaking to the manager."

She headed out to the lobby and almost froze.

The woman standing by the front desk was Jessalyn Parker, one of the two former classmates she'd overheard gossiping about her the day she'd arrived in town. Jessalyn's blue eyes turned cool, and she swished back her honey-blond hair with a shake of her head.

"Oh. Bethany," Jessalyn said, her face falling a bit as if she believed Bethany would block an adoption after that incident in front of the coffee shop. Being a gossip wouldn't stop Bethany from approving Jessalyn as an adopter. But not of Salty solo.

"I hear you're interested in adopting Salty," Bethany said. "He's a bonded pair with Pepper, a beautiful, gentle black Labrador retriever, and we'll only adopt them out together."

"She already told me that," Jessalyn said, turning slightly toward Maya at the front desk. "But Salty—and of course I'd change his name to something befitting him—is really gorgeous. I've always loved Siamese cats. I'll pay extra toward the adoption fee if you'll split them up."

So you don't care that they're a bonded pair? Bethany mentally shook her head. "I'm sorry, but Salty is a package deal. Furever Paws won't separate him and Pepper. They'd be miserable without each other—we learned that fast. Perhaps you'd like to meet Pepper? She's a beauty. Sleek young black Lab, lovely disposition."

"I'm not a dog person," Jessalyn said with a grimace. "Picking up poop? Ew."

I really don't like you, Bethany thought, trying to keep her most neutral expression plastered on her face. "Well, I can ask Laura, one of our staffers, to show you the adoptable cats. She knows our cats inside and out and can give you great info on any you may be interested in. Who's playful, who's more independent, who's a lap cat."

Jessalyn stared at her for a moment. "You're not letting me adopt the Siamese because you heard me talking trash about you. Just admit it. That's *so* high school."

The irony! But Bethany kept her cool, pulling on her years of experience dealing with difficult clients. "Jessalyn, I'm not preventing you from adopting a cat. I'm just explaining the requirements. The shelter will not allow a bonded pair to be separated. We can discuss our other cats, if you'd like." She admittedly wasn't thrilled about the idea of putting any animal in this woman's hands, but not being a particularly nice person didn't mean someone wouldn't be a great pet owner. Case in point: Shane's mother. "Which option would you prefer?"

"Do you have another Siamese who doesn't come with a dog attached?"

"We don't," Bethany said. "But keep checking our

website." She'd offer to call her if any Siamese did come in, but Bethany drew the line at being *overly* helpful to someone who didn't deserve it.

Jessalyn rolled her eyes and huffed out.

Bethany suddenly understood how little she'd had to do with Jessalyn's attitude toward her back in school or when she'd first arrived back in Spring Forest. The woman simply wasn't a kind person. For the first time, Bethany realized that old responses to her weren't about *her* at all. Even when it came to Shane's mother.

"I'm glad she doesn't like dogs," Maya said. "I'd hate for sweet Pepper to go to someone like that. Salty could handle it, of course."

Bethany laughed. "Salty will definitely rule any roost. It's amazing that a cat who's not very friendly is so loving toward a dog. But that's Pepper for you— she can win anyone over." Bethany was about to go back to her office when Josie Whitaker came through the door, her blond hair up in a loose bun, covered muffin tray in her hand.

"Anyone want to try my ham, cheese and pepper frittatas?" Josie asked, setting the tray on the front desk. "I'm perfecting my recipe."

"Ooh," Bethany said. "I would love to."

"Me too," said Maya, taking one and biting into it. "Oh wow. Heavenly!"

Bethany took a bite too. "These are incredible!" She took another bite. "Delicious."

Josie grinned. "Thanks! I made a dozen for a sick friend who I'm visiting tonight, then made two more dozen. I always bring my extras over here since I know everyone loves free food and you guys do such vital, great work. But I admit, I like the praise. And if you could use me around here, I've got a free hour to help out."

"Oh, we could use you, all right," Bethany said, finishing the small frittata too soon. "And thank you for the food and the generous offer to volunteer. In the mood to brush cats? Our volunteer who came in to do that got a migraine and had to leave."

"Sorry about the migraine but brushing cats is exactly what I'd love to do right now," Josie said. "It will help clear my mind."

"Everything okay?" Bethany asked as they headed to the break room, where Josie set out the frittatas and wrote a big note: "Take one! Delicious if I do say so myself! Gluten free, FYI!"

"Okay enough," Josie said as they headed down the hall to the cat room. "I guess I got a little down in the dumps because my daughter might not come visit me on her spring break after all."

"Oh, wow, a college-age daughter. You look so young!"

"Always appreciated hearing that," Josie said with a grin. "I'll be forty-four very soon. I married young and we had a baby right away. Then four years ago, my now ex-husband had an affair with his nurse and left." She sighed and gave Bethany a wistful half smile. "Sorry, that's probably more than you wanted to know. You're either easy to talk to or I'm just an oversharer."

Bethany reached out and gave Josie's hand a squeeze. "It's not oversharing when I really do want to know more about you."

"Anyway, now that I'm an empty nester," Josie continued, "there was really nothing keeping me in Florida. So I moved to Spring Forest for a fresh start right after the birth of my niece and nephew. Plus my aunts, Birdie and Bunny, are here. I'm surrounded by relatives and those precious baby twins, but I have my privacy. And who knows? My fresh start just might include starting my own business—something to do with cooking—and maybe a romance. I have a lot of ideas." Her blue eyes twinkled.

"You've been through so much," Bethany said. "But you seem so positive about the future—so open to possibilities. I wish I were more like that."

Bethany couldn't even imagine opening up her life to adopting a *pet*. So much of her life seemed to be about loss. And dogs? Dogs were so easy to love.

But they got sick. They could run off and not make it home. She couldn't bank on forever with anyone or anything. So she wouldn't.

"The alternative isn't so hot," Josie said. "I'll admit, I've been kinda lonely. I'm thinking it's time for me to shake things up a little. Take a risk or two. All I know for sure is that life has a way of taking a person down unexpected roads."

"Tell me about it," Bethany said, admiring Josie's moxie. "I used to be so afraid of change. I like to know what to expect. But lately I've been realizing the work I've dedicated my life to since I was eighteen is *all about* change and the unexpected— animal rescue."

Josie smiled. "Absolutely. I heard about the dogs and the cat you guys rescued from the backyard breeder. I hope I get to brush Salty today. Rebekah has told me all about him and his salty ways."

Bethany laughed. She had a feeling that if anyone could get Salty to come out of his don't-even-think-about-trying-to-pet-me ways, it would be Josie. "No cat can resist a brushing, especially by the tail and sides of the face. At least I've never met the cat that could."

"Well, let me at him," Josie said. "See you later, Bethany."

Bethany grinned and headed back to her office.

Tonight she'd be helping to babysit Josie's niece and nephew. Plus she'd get to bring Meatball over after work. She'd told the basset hound the good news this morning, and she could have sworn he perked up.

Three babies. A dog. And a home-cooked dinner, this time by her. Talk about change. Bethany was way out of her comfort zone here.

But a big part of her was very excited about all of it.

The other part, the part that sometimes overwhelmed her was scared spitless.

Shane was in the large training yard at Barkyard Boarding, working with his new *thrice*-weekly client: a cute beagle who was very resistant to training. According to his owners, Wexley would not come when you asked him to. He would stop in the middle of the sidewalk and not budge. He ate everything he encountered on the street or at the park. He twice slipped his collar to chase after a chipmunk, scaring his owner to pieces.

The usual tried-and-true methods would not easily work on the tricolored furry bundle of stubbornness. Granted, today was Wexley's first day at Barkyard, but Shane could already see he had his work cut out for him. Beagles were notoriously independent. But Shane knew Wexley's weakness. Cheese sticks—

mozzarella. He had to use the high-value treat rarely, only when he needed to show Wexley that it was worth doing what Shane wanted him to do. There would come a point when the beagle would follow the instruction without even expecting the treat. But that was down the road. Shane liked working with hard-to-train dogs. It made the end result all the more rewarding.

His phone pinged. "Hang on there, Wexley," he told the dog, grabbing his phone. Wexley did not hang on there; instead, he scampered to the other side of the yard to sniff under the trees.

His receptionist had texted him. Your mother's here. Should I send her back?

And then a second later, Oh wait—she's already on her way. Sorry!

Anna pulled open the door that led to the training yard. "I'll wait till you're finished with your furry client," she called over with a wave.

He glanced at the clock on the wall. Wexley's session ended in two minutes. "Wexley, come," he said firmly.

Wexley tilted his head. Shane could see him wondering if he'd get one of those delicious little morsels of mozzarella. The last time he did what the tall man said, he got one.

"Wexley, come," he repeated.

Wexley padded over. Shane knew better than to ask him to sit. That would come next week. "Good, Wexley!" he praised, holding out a small piece of the prized cheese. The beagle gobbled it up, and Shane gave him a pat and scratched under his chin. "Good boy!"

"Really?" came a male voice. "My Wexley? I mean, he's sweet, but does that mean he actually listened?"

Shane turned toward the door and smiled at Henry Mazzario, Wexley's owner, as the man headed over. "Hey, it's his first day. He made good progress on the *come* command. Practice at home as I showed you, using his favorite treats, but stick to that one command. I'll see you in a couple of days for his next session." Wexley was a dog who would benefit from one-on-one training until he had the basic commands down, then he'd schedule Henry to join in on the later sessions—to train *Henry*.

"That cute beagle did go to Shane when he said 'Wexley, come,'" Shane's mother told the man. "I'm a witness."

"Excellent!" Henry said. "Good boy, Wexley! It's the park for you now."

The pair left, and his mother came closer, looking a bit sheepish. Whenever she knew she'd overstepped, gone too far, she always had that expression.

"So I thought we should talk," she said.

"I have fifteen minutes until my next client."

She lifted her chin, now looking less sheepish and more indignant. She didn't like when her son was short with her. But her response was mostly measured. "That's fine. I just want to know what's going on."

"Ah, I thought you were here to apologize. For how you treated Bethany last night. And for running her out of town twelve years ago."

Anna's eyes widened, then she bit her lip and looked away for a moment. "I thought I was looking out for you then, Shane. But I suppose everything I told her would happen if she stuck around happened anyway."

Yeah, it did. He was surprised at his mother's honesty. So he would be honest too.

"I loved her very much," Shane said. "She would have made the terrible situation we had at home much more bearable for me. But instead, I had to deal with being blindsided by the breakup on top of it all."

She bit her lip, her eyes, the same blue as his, heavy with sadness. "I *am* sorry, Shane. I know that doesn't change anything. But I am sorry for everything you went through. I didn't like Bethany then, though. She had a terrible reputation. So who knows?

Maybe I did the right thing, after all, and spared you heartache down the line."

"You didn't," he said. "You were dead wrong and what you did to us, what you said to her, was awful. And by the way, Bethany's supposed reputation was all lies. She didn't deserve that or how you treated her."

Anna sighed, sounding resigned. "I can't change the past, Shane."

"You can treat her with respect now, though. And I expect you to. She's staying with me until Elliot's house—*her* house—is renovated and ready to sell. That could be a couple weeks. And you'll likely run into her coming and going as she checks up on the place."

"So you're dating again?" she asked—nervously.

"We're getting to know each other again is what we're doing."

She waited for Shane to elaborate, but he didn't. And wouldn't. "Well, then. I'm just glad we cleared the air. I'll let you go since you have a client any minute. Bye," she said with a thumbs up as she headed for the door.

He wouldn't call the air *cleared*. Not by a long shot. But it was enough for right now.

"Respect," he called out to her.

He got a wave in response. Dismissive or meant

to indicate "I heard you," he wasn't sure, but he'd said what he'd needed to.

He grabbed his water bottle off the table and took a long chug, turning his thoughts to Bethany. And tonight.

His grand plan.

He had a real opportunity to show Bethany that she was wrong about what she thought she was capable of when it came to being a mother. He'd seen her with Wyatt, how nurturing she'd been the day she'd babysat him. She had it in her. She just had to believe it.

Even if things failed miserably between them, if he accomplished that, if he could give her that belief in herself, he'd feel better about watching her walk out of his life again.

Only he wasn't so sure *he* believed that.

Chapter Thirteen

At six o'clock, Bethany stood at the stove in Shane's kitchen and gave the linguine a stir. She had several pots and pans going for linguine carbonara—simultaneously cooking bacon, peas and a scrumptious cream sauce. The salad was dressed and tossed, the garlic bread just about done. Dinner would be ready in five minutes, and the Whitakers weren't due till 7:00, so she and Shane would have a good hour to enjoy the meal with just Wyatt around before the house got much fuller with triple joyful baby shrieks.

Meatball was in his bed at the far end of the kitchen, half snoozing, half sniffing the air. She'd brought his favorite chew toy, which was under his chin.

"This is much better than my office, huh, Meatball?" she asked the basset hound. At the sound of his name, he glanced up at her, then rested his head back on the rim of the bed. He did look happier, even if wasn't easy to tell when bassets *were* happy. She reached into her pocket and pulled out her baggie of treats—did anyone in animal rescue not have that baggie in their pocket at all times?—and gave Meatball a liver snap, his favorite.

"Something smells way too good," Shane said, coming into the kitchen with Wyatt in his arms. "I'm a decent cook but I've never made the air smell like that, even though I make bacon nearly every day."

She smiled. "It's the addition of the tangy cream sauce and the garlic bread too."

"Wyatt, do you want to try a little bit of linguine with peas?" Shane asked his son, setting him in the high chair. "I'll cut up the pasta in tiny pieces." He turned to Bethany. "I just gave him his bottle and he had a jar of baby food, but how can I deny him something that smells that amazing?"

She grinned, puffing up a bit at the praise. It had been a long time since she'd made dinner for anyone. Though she liked cooking, it always seemed like a lot of trouble for one person. She had cereal for dinner a little too often.

Her chest clenched a bit as she watched Shane buckle up Wyatt in the high chair. In another life, if their past had played out differently, he would be her husband, their baby would be in that high chair, this would be their house. The way she'd felt about Shane back then would have crushed her fears about family life and having children. He would have made her feel like she could be mother of the year.

I could have had all this.

But twelve years of a very different life had made her sure she couldn't have "all this" after all. So many disappointments had reinforced those walls around her heart and head that she'd started building long before she left town—the walls only Shane had ever breached. There had been other attempts, including the two relationships that failed spectacularly. Scattered before and after them were a bunch of very short-term romances that either dashed her hopes when she'd actually gotten excited about someone who didn't reciprocate her enthusiasm or when she realized the guy wasn't for her—a cat hater, rude to the waiter, ogled the waitress, ranted, spoke in monologues and barely asked her a question about herself. And losing the shelter she ran hurt badly, the final nail in the coffin of her willingness to open herself up to another rejection.

Everything ended in goodbye. And sometimes, she didn't even get to say goodbye. Like when she'd lost her mother, who'd died suddenly in an accident.

Bethany closed her eyes for a second and tried to will all these heavy, sad thoughts away. She looked at sweet Meatball, hoping he'd cheer her up as he always did. But she suddenly felt very out of place here, in Shane's kitchen, making him dinner. Thinking about how she would set aside a tiny, baby-proofed portion of linguine in a bit of sauce, without the soft bacon, for Wyatt.

She shut off the oven and took out the garlic bread, then drained the pasta and poured it into the big pan of sauce simmering with the bacon and peas. "Can I ask you something a little on the personal side?"

"Anything," he said.

"Actually, I have two questions."

"Ask away," he said. "And what can I help with? Give me a job."

"You can bring over the salad and the garlic bread. I've got the pasta."

He got up, his long, muscular frame practically filling the large kitchen. Damn, he was sexy. When she'd arrived here with Meatball a half hour ago, he'd clearly just come from the shower because his dark hair had been damp, his feet were bare and he'd smelled incredible. For a moment, she'd just stared at him, unable to look away, flickers of their night in the vacant office at the shelter going through her mind.

How could she possibly guard herself against a

man she couldn't stop wanting, couldn't stop thinking about?

Shane sliced up the bread and put it in a basket, then brought the salad and bread to the table.

"Ba!" Wyatt said, giving his tray table a little pound with his fist.

"Ba!" Shane said back with a smile.

Bethany got a little plastic bowl and Wyatt's blue spoon and dished up his small portion, the linguine cut up, the peas pushed in a bit to ensure they weren't a choking hazard. "This look okay?" she asked, bringing it over.

"Perfect," he said, taking the bowl.

She brought over the big bowl of pasta and set it in the center of the table. "So here's my first question. Did you let your ex-wife know that someone is staying here with you?"

"Yes, actually," he said. "When she and her boyfriend dropped off Wyatt earlier."

Bethany paused with a piece of garlic bread in her hand. "She's okay with a strange woman living in your house with Wyatt?"

"You're not a stranger to her."

"I'm not?" she asked, heaping some salad on her plate.

"Nina was a year behind us in high school. When I told her you were staying here, she said, 'Oh, I remember Bethany Robeson. Really nice girl. She tutored me in Algebra II before the midterm and final.' She also said she once overheard a jerk lying through his teeth about going on a date with you the night before at the exact time you were with her at the library, helping her study."

"Wait, your ex-wife is Nina Welling?"

He nodded.

"Huh. I did tutor her. I couldn't get her grade above a C, but at least she didn't fail!"

He smiled. "She said you saved her from flunking out."

"Small world." And that took one thing off her mind—wondering if Shane's ex was one of the townspeople with preconceived notions about her. She certainly didn't want to create problems for Shane with his ex by staying at his house. She shook her head and helped herself to the pasta. "Hmm, this is pretty good, if I do say so myself." She smiled, remembering Josie had written that today about her frittatas.

Shane took a bite too. "Better than pretty good. Really delicious." He turned to Wyatt and held out his little spoon. "Open, something yummy coming!"

Wyatt stared at the spoon.

"He's either going to bat it out of my hand, open his mouth, or turn away. It's anyone's guess."

"I'll vote for bat it out of your hand. I saw a baby do that at the coffee shop the other day."

He laughed. "I'd put money on that one if you hadn't made this, Bethany. Wyatt can spot great food a mile away."

She laughed too and watched as Wyatt leaned his head forward a bit—and opened his mouth.

"I know my boy," Shane said, giving Wyatt the spoonful.

Wyatt kind of tilted his head, then opened his mouth again.

Bethany grinned. "He does like it!"

"Of course, he does," Shane said. "I started him on solids last month, and once he got used to jarred baby food he started eyeing my plate. We might have a future chef sitting right here."

She couldn't help but notice the "we." Shane always included her, always managed to make her feel warm and fuzzy inside, despite her usual lack of optimism about love and family.

After a couple more small spoonfuls, Wyatt turned his attention to batting at the little springy mobile at the side of his tray.

Shane took another bite of his own pasta, then grabbed a piece of garlic bread. "And what was your second question?"

Oh yeah. *That*. "Did you talk to your mom today?

I'm planning on going to Elliot's house tomorrow on my lunch break, so just in case I run into your mom, I thought I'd ask." She was pretty sure she already knew the answer, though.

Yes, and she said she still hates your guts and thinks even less of you for getting Elliot Bradley's house.

Of course, even if Anna did feel that way, had said that, Shane wouldn't tell her so. He'd sugarcoat the truth to be kind. But Bethany had had her fill of people thinking she was "less than" in Spring Forest. It couldn't really get to her anymore; she'd hardened against it long ago, but that didn't mean it had no effect at all.

Especially when it came to Shane's mother.

Shane looked at her and nodded. "I did talk to her. She apologized for what she did twelve years ago. She said she really thought she was helping me by making sure you didn't derail my plans, but she realized it wouldn't have mattered if you'd stayed in my life or not because I didn't go away to college anyway."

Bethany tried not to think about the day his mother had come to her apartment, all Anna had said. She could still remember every word, the disdain on the woman's face. "She still doesn't like me. I can kind of hear that in what you're not saying."

He let out a sigh. "Again, Bethany, there is nothing about you not to like. You're sunlight. *Sunlight*. If someone doesn't like you, there's something wrong with them."

Unexpected tears pricked her eyes. *She* was sunlight? Bethany certainly wouldn't describe herself as radiant or cheerful.

"Think about what you do for those dogs and cats at Furever Paws," he said. "Birdie needed you—you said yes. I needed you—you said yes. You're essential, Bethany Robeson."

She felt like he wrapped a warm blanket around her. "Okay, I'm a little too touched by what you just said."

He reached for her hand and held it. "Sunlight, Bethany. Just remember that."

She gave his hand a squeeze back, wanting to fling herself into his arms and stay there.

"You always make me feel so good," she said. "Hopeful. Like everything will be okay."

"Good. Everyone needs a person like that in their life. I'm glad it's me."

"Who's that for you?" she asked.

"This little dude," he said, pointing his fork at Wyatt, who batted at his mobile and yelled out a joyful *ba*. "Everything *has* to be okay for him, so I try to make sure it is. Keeps me on track."

"That's really lovely," she said, realizing she was staring at him kind of moonily. Like she used to in history class.

"I used to think like you do," he said. "That I couldn't be a good dad because of my father. But if I want to be the father Wyatt needs and deserves, I have to step up. Plain and simple. *I* choose. Not my past. Not my own dad. Not my mom. No one and nothing decides who I am but me. And Wyatt."

She took that all in. She knew, intellectually, that he was right. But everyone's perception of *who she was* was so ingrained. Had been for so long.

Wyatt let out a burp, eliciting giggles from her and Shane, which helped change the subject and lighten the mood in the kitchen. *So thank you, Wyatt Dupree.*

Their bellies full, their plates just about empty, dinner was over. Shane insisted on cleaning up the kitchen since she'd cooked. She played a couple rounds of peekaboo with Wyatt, getting a *ba!* and a big gummy smile.

You are so precious. But you scare the bejesus out of me. You really do.

So does your dad.

Shane, scrubbing the bacon pan with his hands full of suds, looked over at her. "Oh, hey, would you mind changing him while I take care of this?" he asked. "His changing table is across from his crib in the nursery. He could definitely use a fresh set of PJs for his big playdate."

Bethany froze for just a split second. Change him? She swallowed. "I've never changed a baby before. You probably think that's odd, that I could get to age thirty without ever changing a diaper, but remember, the first time I ever held a baby was Wyatt a few days ago."

"Well, you don't have nieces and nephews, so it's not that odd," he said. "But I believe you're up for the challenge. You did a great job of watching him that morning I had the training session. You even fed him."

True. Two firsts.

"Okay, I'm on it," she said. She unbuckled Wyatt from his high chair and reached out to scoop him up, but his face crumpled. And he let out a shriek.

She stepped back, biting her lip. "It's me, Bethany!" she said in a singsong voice. "You just loved my linguine carbonara!"

She tried to pick him up again, but he started bawling.

It was like the baby knew she was afraid of him. All eighteen pounds of baby. Her heart plummeted.

"Oh no, sorry, Shane. What did I do wrong?"

"Nothing at all," he said, rinsing his hands and

drying them. "He's just being what he is—a baby. Unpredictable. Could be gassy. It's not you."

It's me. He knows I'm brand-new at all of this. He can sense it, that I don't know the first thing about changing a baby. He doesn't want me near him!

Bethany Rae Robeson, take charge, she told herself. *You've won over aggressive, scared dogs. You're gonna let a little human best you?*

She reached for him again. "I'm going to get you changed and ready for friends!" she said in a perky voice.

Wyatt screamed at the top of his lungs. "Waaaaaaah! Waaah-waaaah!" His face was turning red.

"Why don't I finish up in here and you take Wyatt," she said, trying not to let her disappointment show on her face.

What do you expect, though? You're always saying you're not cut out for motherhood. Now Shane can see it for himself. She *didn't* get to decide. She didn't have it in her. And Wyatt knew it. At seven months old.

Her stomach churning, Bethany started stacking the dishes and grabbing platters.

"He's just being a fusspot," he said. "Please don't take it personally."

"I thought I was *way* over people not liking me. But Wyatt's special. Of course I want him to like me."

That was it, she realized. When he'd easily gone into her arms the first time she'd tried to hold him, when he'd happily let her feed him his bottle—she'd felt such a boost. Like, *Ha, Jessalyn Parker types. This little guy adores me, so there!*

He shot her a look of compassion as he scooped up Wyatt, the tears instantly stopping. "Wyatt thinks you're awesome. Right, Wyatt? Bethany is great."

"Ba!" Wyatt said with his gummy smile.

Bethany tried to smile back, but the tears and get-the-hell-away-from-me screaming had gotten to her.

"Be right back," Shane said, his gaze warm on her.

Bethany nodded, focusing on filling the dishwasher and wiping down the counters. At least the kitchen was clean now.

The doorbell rang just as Shane came back down with Wyatt in his arms, dressed in cute blue-and-white-striped PJs with tiny dinosaurs all over.

Were the Whitaker twins going to scream bloody murder if she tried to pick them up too?

The moment the door opened, little Lily Whitaker took one look at Bethany and started fussing, her brother looking like he might start too.

Good Lord, I'm baby repellent!

Now Bethany wanted to cry too.

Chapter Fourteen

Shane's grand plan had tanked big-time tonight. Instead of proving to Bethany that she was meant for family life, he'd done the opposite. Well, the babies had. Wyatt had been fussy off and on for the next two hours. Lily and Lucas were distracted by their fun soft play mat but they had their moments too, and unfortunately, a few of those very fussy moments had coincided with Bethany attempting to play with them.

She'd been a trouper for the two hours they were babysitting the Whitaker twins, getting down on the floor for crawl time, calming down one twin while he calmed down Wyatt, keeping her voice light and baby-friendly even though she looked like she wanted to run far, far away.

Finally, Rebekah and Grant returned to pick up Lily and Lucas, and Bethany breathed a visible sigh of relief once the door was shut behind them.

"Well, I know I'm not cut out for triplets," she said, dropping down on the sofa. "I saw how hard *one* baby can be."

"One baby isn't that hard," he said, even though it was a total lie. Of course it was hard. But definitely easier than three so not a total lie in context of their conversation.

Yeah, keep rationalizing, he told himself glumly.

"There's so much to know, to consider, to worry about," she said. "Even the light pressing of the peas in the pasta to prevent choking."

"Well, you thought to do that without me having to say a thing," he said, brightening. "A perfect example of how you *do* understand a baby's needs. Someone else might not have realized a basically soft pea could use a little squishing for a seven-month-old."

He could see her considering that. Bethany was thoughtful—in all ways. And being thoughtful was a huge part of taking care of a baby.

"Babies cry," he said. "They get really fussy. Just

because I'm his dad and he knows me doesn't mean Wyatt doesn't scream his head off with me sometimes. Ask anyone at the grocery store last week."

She gave a smile. "Maybe."

"Not maybe. Definitely. Help me get this guy to bed?"

Shane loved getting Wyatt to bed. Sitting in the glider, telling him a story—sometimes made up, sometimes from a book—cuddling *his* baby, snuggled safely in his arms. He'd look down at Wyatt and be so moved by him, by fatherhood, that he'd have to stop the story and collect himself, take a breath. Then standing over the crib, watching the tiny chest go up and down, up and down, the bow lips giving a quirk. The entire world was in that crib.

All that was such a big part of who Shane was, and he wanted Bethany to be part of it. Even if she didn't see herself as a mother.

Because you want her to be part of your life.

"I'm not sure I'd be much help," she said.

"Here," he said. "You take him. You'll see that earlier was just a fluke."

He held out Wyatt to Bethany, fully expecting— okay, *hoping*—that the baby would sweetly gaze up at her with his big sleepy blue eyes…but Wyatt started to cry again.

Then scream.

Oh hell. Kiddo, you're not helping me out here.

"He's just overtired," Shane said. "Which is my fault. He stayed up past his usual bedtime." Which was true. A baby's schedule was everything, but sometimes there were curve balls and fun playdates and a little flexibility was required. Not from the baby, though.

Wyatt shrieked all the way up the stairs, Bethany following, her expression tight.

In the nursery, Shane changed Wyatt's diaper, then sat down on the love seat by the window. He had a chance to turn things around, and he was going for it.

"How about you pick a book to read," he asked her. "Anything on his shelves."

She went over to the bookcase and pulled out a book. *"Dewey's Big Adventure."* She held it up. "Cute frog on the cover. I can read it to him, if that's okay."

He relaxed at that. "Both Duprees would like that very much."

She glanced at Wyatt, lying against Shane's chest, and sat down beside him, holding up the book so Wyatt could see the illustrations. "'Hi, my name is Dewey. I'm a frog. But not just any old frog. I have a secret superpower! I can hop across a pond with one leap.'"

The baby let out a giant yawn, his little eyes drooping.

Bethany continued to read about Dewey saving the day with his great leaping abilities.

By the time she got to page four, Wyatt was fast asleep.

"Aww, he's out cold," she said, gently closing the book.

He smiled, looking down at his sleeping son. "Thanks for reading to him."

"Another first. I've definitely never read a bedtime story to a sleepy baby before."

He wanted to just sit there, holding his son, next to Bethany, but he was pretty sure she could use a break from the baby world she'd been immersed in over the past couple of hours. He stood, gently swaying Wyatt in his arms. "Hopefully he'll transfer into his crib without a peep."

He did.

"Well, it's been a really long day," she said. "So I think I'll just turn in."

Oh hell again.

So much for his grand plan. A grand *flop*.

He was about to ask her if she wanted to have some tea or coffee on the deck, but she'd hurried out of the nursery before he could say a word.

And he heard her door close with a definite click.

Give her space, his instincts said.

Even if it's very hard not to knock, to ask if she's okay, to offer to hold her.

At just after eleven that night, Bethany could faintly hear the shower running next door in Shane's bedroom, where he had an en suite bathroom. He'd gotten spit up on a few times tonight, mostly because he'd been the one doing most of the baby holding. At some points he'd had a baby in each arm.

She'd tried, though. Nervous as she'd been after Wyatt's meltdown, then how the Whitaker twins had greeted her with shrieks of terror too, she'd tried hard. She'd played round after round of peekaboo because Lily seemed to like it, but then the adorable baby girl started to cry, her face turning red, and Bethany couldn't comfort her despite all the tricks Shane had told her to try. Bouncing, swaying, rocking, singing, making funny faces, holding the baby vertically, holding the baby horizontally, patting the girl's back for a burp.

Shane had been so good with the babies, all three. Yeah, he'd been a father for seven months and knew what he was doing, but he was great at fatherhood, a natural. He made caring for babies seem so effortless.

If she were really honest with herself, she'd admit

to hoping she'd be proven wrong about herself tonight, that she had some untapped maternal instincts that would make her great with babies. Nope.

"Waaah. Waah-waaah!"

Wyatt was crying. Bethany glanced at the time on her phone. She could still hear the shower running.

If she knew Shane, and she did, he had a baby monitor in the bathroom with him and would cut his shower short to check on Wyatt.

He shouldn't have to do that with an extra pair of ears and hands here tonight: hers. After all he'd done for her, she should go help.

Would making Wyatt cry harder help, though?

Go, she told herself.

"I'm coming, Wyatt," she called out, hurrying out from her room and into the nursery.

Wyatt was crying and squirming in his crib, reaching out his arms.

"Aww, I've got you, little guy," she said, picking him up. "What's wrong? Tummy bothering you? I can help while your daddy's in the shower, okay?"

She held Wyatt vertically against her chest the way Shane had shown her, rubbing his back with big circles, a light pressure. She walked around the room, to the windows, rocking and swaying and back-rubbing—and the crying stopped. Wyatt's eyes got droopy.

Whoa.

She kept it up walking and gently rocking the baby until he was clearly asleep again.

Aww, she thought, loving the soft weight of him in her arms, the baby-shampoo scent of his hair.

"I heard him cry from the bathroom monitor and got out of the shower," Shane said. "But you beat me to it. Thank you."

He stood in the doorway, hair dripping, a line of water making its way down the center of his muscled chest, towel tied across his hips.

Bethany swallowed.

She couldn't take her eyes off him.

"Looks like you got him right back to sleep," he said. "You can put him in the crib," he added, stepping into the room. Still with just that towel across his hips. "He just might go without waking up."

"I'll try," she managed to say. She turned and walked over to the crib, looking down at the sweet baby boy, his lip rising on one side. He was definitely fast asleep. She did not want to be the cause of him waking up. She gently put him down and held her breath.

One tiny arm lifted in a fist alongside his head, the eyes remaining closed. His chest rose up and down, up and down.

She'd done it! Soothed him back to sleep, then put him in his crib again.

"I feel like I redeemed myself just a little," she said. "Okay a lot. Phew."

Shane smiled and then took her hand and led her out of the room, turning off the light and leaving the door ajar. Once they were outside, he did not let go of her hand. "Thank you for caring for him."

He was so close. An inch away. So touchable.

"Did your shower get interrupted?" she managed to ask, trying not to stare as another bead of water slid down his chest. "Shampoo still in your hair?"

His gaze was intensely focused on her. "I was done. Just letting the hot water take away the long day. You know?"

"Oh, I know."

He looked at her. She looked at him, and once again, they both moved forward at the same time.

This time she backed him against the wall, furiously kissing him, her hands in his damp hair, then all over his bare chest. His hands were on either side of her face, kissing her so passionately, and when he reached to lift her T-shirt, the towel fell.

"Didn't need it anyway," he whispered.

"Nope," she whispered back, her mouth on his neck. He smelled delicious.

He flung off her shirt, then wiggled off her PJ bottoms. He looked down at her, almost naked except for her white cotton underwear. "I think we should match, don't you?" he asked, trailing kisses along her collarbone as he peeled off the underwear.

She could barely think, let alone find her voice.

"Mmm," she whispered, leaning her head back, wanting to give him all the room he needed to never stop kissing every inch of her body.

He took her hand and led her into his bedroom. She hadn't been in here before. He had a huge bed, leather headboard, lots of soft-looking pillows and a down comforter.

"We can't seem to stop doing this," she said, licking his ear, her hand on his broad shoulder. Every part of her was tingling.

He groaned and picked her up. "I definitely can't," he said, placing her on the bed.

He lay down on top of her, taking both her hands and raising them over her head, kissing her passionately. Then he slowly moved down her body, his lips trying to get everywhere, his hands roaming.

You could let yourself have this, a little voice said. Even if she was leaving soon. Even if this was just for now.

"Maybe you should think about staying in Spring Forest," Shane whispered.

She froze, and she felt him freeze, too. He had to be just caught up in the moment. Right?

"Maybe I shouldn't have said that out loud." He moved back up so that they were at eye level, his hands gentle on her face. "Dammit."

"It's better you did," she said. "We need the reminder to be careful with ourselves."

He looked directly into her eyes. "I want you, Bethany. I always have. This is my second chance, and second chances don't come along often. I'm not throwing it away. Is it a risk? Yeah, it is. But one worth taking."

She didn't put herself at risk anymore. It was how she lived her life. The *tenet* of her life.

"I don't know, Shane," she said, her voice uneven. "Staying here was never part of the plan."

"*We* weren't part of the plan. But here we are. Naked in bed. Things change, evolve, grow."

She wished she could explain that this didn't feel truly real. It certainly didn't feel like something that could last. She could be here with him like this because Spring Forest was temporary, *he* was temporary. Meatball was temporary. She knew that, and she never lost sight of it. Shane wasn't hers. Meatball wasn't hers. Wyatt certainly wasn't hers.

"I've been very focused on the plan I *do* have," she said. "From the moment I got that shocking phone call from Elliot's lawyer about the house, I've had a plan. Coming, going, funding a new animal rescue where I live. When I hang on to that plan, everything else doesn't overwhelm me. Things like whether or not Elliot is my father. How I was raised. The reputation I had in middle and high school. My ambivalence about my mom. Being in this town. Having to leave you and start fresh somewhere else. If I just focus on selling the house and the goal of building a new shelter, I'm okay."

He seemed to be taking all that in. "But this—what we have between us—can help make all that easier. That's what partnership is all about. Comfort. Support. Helping each other through. You're going to give this up? I don't see how you can, Bethany."

Her heart squeezed. He didn't really understand. That was a good thing. It meant he was open to love and risk, despite everything he'd been through. His family life. His old dreams having to shift suddenly. His divorce.

She wasn't.

Why was it so hard for her when people like Josie and Birdie and Shane could still believe in love despite their losses? She'd given up on it so hard that it wasn't something she wanted anymore. Or dreamed about. She'd closed the door and locked it.

She slipped out of his bed and quickly dressed. She needed to go back in the guest room.

"Bethany," he said, but she could hear the resignation in his voice.

In a week, a week and a half, the house would be finished and ready for sale. Birdie had been feeling out possible replacements for both her and Rebekah "just in case" and had two good contenders. Bethany wouldn't be leaving Birdie in the lurch. She wouldn't even have to stay in town while it was on the market; a real estate agent could handle that for her. And once the place sold, she'd use the money to fund her dream.

The dream you're actually now living, a small voice pointed out. *You're the interim director of Furever Paws. If Rebekah did decide to come back to work full time, you could be assistant director. You're already working in the rescue that would be the model for the one you would build.*

You're living your dream life. The life you once thought you could have.

She hadn't really thought of that before.

But there was nothing scary about starting an animal rescue center. She'd have the money. She had the experience, the training and she was ready to be her own Birdie and Bunny.

Scary was Shane Dupree and his baby son.

Scary was how attached she was becoming to a droopy-eared basset hound named Meatball.

Scary was the prospect of finding out who her father was once and for all—or learning that she'd never be able to know.

What wasn't scary? Leaving Spring Forest. That would just hurt like hell.

Chapter Fifteen

At six forty in the morning, Bethany pulled into the lot at Furever Paws, Meatball beside her, buckled in. Shane's regular sitter was back in town, so he was all set for childcare during his early-morning training class.

Things had been awkward, to say the least, between them as they'd passed each other in his upstairs hallway just a half hour ago, Bethany fresh out of the shower, her towel tight around her chest, her hair wet around her shoulders.

He'd stared at her for a moment, and she could see he wanted to say something, but he didn't, just nodded and faintly smiled and kept going.

She'd had to stand there for a second to let the intensity calm down a bit.

When she'd gone downstairs, he'd been in the kitchen, making breakfast, but she said she'd just grab a bagel from the break room.

She wanted to tell him how sorry she was that she was too long-set in her ways as a woman alone. But she knew Shane didn't want to hear that. He wanted to hear that she was staying, that she'd choose him and Wyatt.

If only it were that easy. But there was nothing easy about fear. And Bethany had a phobia about letting love into her life.

She felt eyes on her and looked over at Meatball. His soulful gaze almost made her want to cry. *You've been through the wringer too and so you're shy, not so trusting of people. I get it.* Yet at the same time, she was working hard at bringing him out of his shell. Like Shane had been trying to do with her.

She was asking more of Meatball than she was willing to give herself.

She leaned her head back and let out a sigh.

It was time to shift her thoughts to the rescue center. To focus on the fundraising plan. All those dogs in foster homes, all those puppies about to come into the world—Furever Paws needed to provide for them till they all found their forever homes. She wouldn't run Furever Paws for much longer, but while she was there, she needed to do her best to get this situation taken care of.

"So Meatball," she said, "we'll go for a nice walk and get your exercise in, and then I'll serve you breakfast. How's that? And I got a text last night that a wonderful group did a pet toy collection that's set to arrive this morning, and that means a new chew toy for you."

Meatball leaned his head against her shoulder, and she almost gasped, her heart melting.

"Why are you so sweet?" she whispered, both her hands in his soft fur. "You're the best, Meatball. Someone out there doesn't know how lucky they are that they're going to have you."

She gave him one last nuzzle, then got out of her SUV, Meatball hopping down beside her. A car pulled into the lot, and she turned to shield her eyes from the glorious spring morning sun. It was Rebekah Whitaker, holding a covered tray.

"Twins woke up at like 5:02," Rebekah said, "and one woke up in the night, which woke up the other, which makes for two tired parents this morning. Josie is babysitting right now so I thought I'd check in here. Oh, and she made chocolate-coconut muffins."

"Ooh, I will definitely take one of those," Bethany said. "Good to be here early because they'll be gone in seconds. You're so dedicated to come here when you have baby care—you must be exhausted."

"I am. But I always am. And I love this place. I mean, who wouldn't be dedicated to dogs like this beautiful creature?" she added, leaning down to pet Meatball under his chin.

Bethany smiled and they headed inside. She let Meatball into the fenced dog run, then she and Rebekah went to the break room. Bethany made a pot of coffee, and they each took a muffin, ahhing at how good they were.

Once the coffee was ready, they sat down at the table, Bethany able to see Meatball out the window, sniffing away and ambling after a bird. "Please tell Josie I'd pay a million dollars for a dozen of these muffins," Bethany said, taking another bite of confection perfection. "Not that I have a million dollars."

Rebekah laughed. "We're so lucky to have her right on the property. Amazing cook, amazing with babies."

"Then there's me. Terrible with babies. Maybe I shouldn't tell you that *after* I already helped babysit your twins." She sighed—hard.

"I'm sure you're wonderful with babies," Rebekah said. "Anyone who loves animals the way you do has a heart of pure gold. I think you just caught the twins on a bad day. When the mood strikes, babies cry and screech and can make even the most patient of saints feel awful. Lily has a really close bond with her dad, and there was a stretch where she would scream her head off when he'd try to hand her to me. I felt like dog-doo! But I quickly learned that kind of thing has nothing to do with me. It's fickle baby stuff."

"Wyatt did let me soothe him back to sleep last night," Bethany said, her chest unclenching and her shoulders unbunching. "He's so precious. And watching him and the twins crawl around and giggle at one another—they were so sweet. I could watch babies play all day, and I never thought I'd say that. Of course, the screeching and crying when I come near them is another story, but—"

Tears pooled in Rebekah's eyes. She put down the muffin she was holding, her face crumpling.

Bethany reached out a hand. "Hey, what's wrong?"

"I love Furever Paws," Rebekah said. "My heart is here. But I want to be home with my babies. I *just* had them. And they were in the NICU for a while and I was so scared. When I have a sitter, I feel like I'm supposed to be here. But I want to be home. All the time." She covered her face with her hands.

"Rebekah, you need to do what feels right. What you really want deep down. And if that's being home full time with Lily and Lucas, then please, please, please don't feel a second's worry about Furever

Paws. You know everyone here is dedicated. You're not letting anyone down."

"That's what Birdie said. And Bunny when I spoke to her yesterday when she called from somewhere on the road." She took in a breath and wiped at her eyes. "But you're only here temporarily, right? I'd feel so much better about leaving Furever Paws if I knew you were permanent."

Permanent.

"I was never planning to stay past the sale of Elliot's house," Bethany said.

Rebekah tilted her head. "Oh—I thought you and Shane had gotten serious. I mean, the two of you seem like a *very* tight couple."

Last night's painful conversation echoed in her head. Shane asking her to stay in Spring Forest. Bethany trying to explain why she was leaving. "I was never planning on the two of us picking up where we left off twelve years ago. We're not remotely the same people we were back then, and yet everything that was between us back then is even stronger now." She shook her head. "But…"

"Hey, sounds like we're both being pulled in unexpected directions. So I'll just throw your own great advice back to you. You need to do what feels right, what you really want deep down. And I need to go home to my twins and to have some of Josie's amazing blueberry pancakes." She stood up and held out her arms.

Bethany stood too and gave Rebekah a tight hug, then they went out in the dog run. "I'll keep you updated on things here, but only if you want."

"Well, until I make a final decision about whether or not I'll be coming back, I'll still be here part-time." She bent down and petted Meatball. "See you later, long ears."

Bethany smiled and watched Rebekah leave through the gate and head back to her car.

Knowing someone else was being pulled in two directions made her feel a little better, not that she'd wish this feeling on anyone.

I thought you and Shane had gotten serious…

She looked out the window at Meatball, now lying down on the grass, head on his paws. She'd have to say goodbye to Meatball when he was ready for adoption. And she'd have to say goodbye to Shane. She had once before. But this time, she wasn't newly eighteen and hopeful because she was so madly in love.

She knew better.

But as she gazed at Meatball, getting up to trail slowly after another bird pecking at the ground, her heart started clenching again, her shoulders rebunching.

I don't know anything, she thought.

* * *

On her lunch break, Bethany took Meatball for his half-mile walk, noticing that he was picking up the pace—a great sign that their work was paying off. He'd only lost two pounds since Bethany had started working at Furever Paws, but that was still significant for a dog. He had a ways to go, but they'd get there together.

We'll definitely get there, she told herself, cheering herself on as she pulled into the driveway at Elliot's house. She glanced to the right, hoping she wouldn't see Anna's SUV in the driveway, but there it was.

Darn.

And there was the woman herself, coming up the sidewalk on the left, leading Princess on her pink leash with a new rhinestone collar. She couldn't possibly miss seeing Bethany in her car.

In fact, her steely blue gaze was fixed on Bethany through the lowered window. The woman frowned, then moved her features into a more neutral, almost pleasant expression.

Anna stopped at the car. No barking from the Chihuahua, so it looked like Shane had done some good work with the little dog over the past days. "I was wrong to interfere in your and Shane's life that day you both graduated from high school," Anna said. "I really believed the two of you were wrong for each other. I'm sure you still are, but he's a grown man and makes his own decisions."

Good Godfrey. Bethany knew Shane's mother had been through a lot and she was *very* tightly wound, but enough was enough. If Bethany wanted answers, she had to ask questions.

"Let me ask you, Mrs. Dupree. Why is it that you don't like me? Because of who my mother was? Because we lived in a shabby apartment above a bar?"

Anna's blue eyes reflected her surprise at the question. "Yes, on both points, to be honest. I believed you would distract Shane from his goals, but all that blew up to high heaven anyway, so..."

"And your coolness to me now?" Bethany asked. "Just carryover from twelve years ago?" She really was curious.

She knew it wasn't because Anna had been close to Elliot's wife and Bethany was a reminder of the affair; Shane had said his mother hadn't liked *either* Bradley, just as she didn't like anyone except her dog.

"It's time for Princess's snack," Anna said, and turned and walked toward her house.

Bethany shook her head. There had to be a reason for the woman's special brand of coldness, particularly when her own son was Bethany's champion. The whispers and rumor mill about Bethany had died down very quickly since her return to Spring Forest. Honestly, no one really cared about an old scandal that had no effect on their lives, and now people knew Bethany Robeson as the director of Furever Paws, not the daughter of "that woman running around with a married man."

Bethany did still get a few stares in town. Sometimes a potential adopter slash former classmate would see her around Furever Paws and do a double take, but the moment after that double take always seemed to include the realization that twelve years had passed and whatever the person thought of Bethany then couldn't possibly have any bearing on *now*.

Then there was Shane's mother.

Then again, Anna hadn't liked Shane's ex-wife, who Bethany remembered as a very kind person. Maybe Anna simply didn't think *anyone* was good enough for Shane.

Or maybe the woman knew something. Something she didn't like.

Bethany got out of her car and marched straight up to the Dupree front door before she could change her mind and rang the bell.

Now Princess barked, her little nails clicking on the front entry along with Anna's footsteps. The door opened. Anna's eyes narrowed and her chin lifted.

"I have a question for you, if you don't mind," Bethany said. She might as well ask.

Anna raised an eyebrow.

"Do you dislike me, because someone, maybe Elliot himself, told you that I *am* his daughter and for some reason that bothers you?"

Anna just stared at her. Said absolutely nothing. Her expression didn't change.

Keep going, Bethany told herself. *Try again. A different tactic. Get through to her.*

"I've never known who my father is, Mrs. Dupree. Think about how hard that would be for a child, a teenager, a grown woman. If you do know, you could help put that burning question behind me, help me find peace with it."

She and Elliot had been neighbors for decades. Maybe they'd *become* friends in the past bunch of years.

"Not only do I not know who your father is," Anna said, "but Elliot didn't know either. That's all I care to say on the subject." With that she closed the door.

What did *that* mean?

Elliot didn't know either. So Anna *did* know something. Elliot must have opened up to her.

But if he didn't know, why would he have left Bethany the house?

This just didn't make sense. None of it.

But twice in the space of two minutes, Anna Dupree had walked away from her, this last time closing the door in her face. She clearly had no interest in talking any further. Bethany would let the conversation end for now. But she'd be back. Shane's mother *knew* something. Bethany wanted to know what.

Determined to finish this at some point, she crossed over onto her property and knocked on the front door.

Harris Vega, the house flipper extraordinaire, greeted her warmly. "Bethany! Nice to see you again. You'll be surprised at how fast my team and I are moving. I think we're going to get the work done in a week. The bones of this house are good."

A week. That was all the time she'd have left with Shane and Wyatt and Meatball. With Furever Paws.

This is what you wanted, Bethany, she reminded herself. But it grabbed her by the heart and twisted, nonetheless. Twisted hard.

"Wow, that's faster than I thought," she said.

Harris nodded, his dark hair and eyes sparkling in the bright sunshine. Bethany figured he was no older than late twenties, but he was so accomplished and successful. "If you come by tomorrow afternoon, you'll see the upstairs bathroom all finished. No more pink sink and tub." He smiled. "You might be surprised to hear I did have a client who specifically asked for a pink sink and tub, but it was a very modern approach—all iridescent and marble surrounds. Want to see what we've accomplished upstairs so far?"

She really just wanted to get far away from here. From this house. From next door.

"You know what? I'll just come when you're done. It'll be great to see the magic at its full effect."

He gave her another warm smile and headed back in.

Bethany glanced over at the Dupree house, sure she saw someone darting away from the window, shielded by the curtain.

She couldn't get away from here fast enough.

Except the moment she drove away, toward Furever Paws, she remembered that when the time came to leave for good, getting away fast meant saying some very painful goodbyes. She and Shane had a week left in each other's lives. A week left of staying in the same house. But she'd have to change how things were between them. No more cozy breakfasts or family-like dinners. No more babysitting—unless of course he was in a real jam. It was just too emotionally hard on her.

No more sleeping together.

No more living in a fantasy world when she was only going to break her own heart after reality came knocking.

Chapter Sixteen

Shane waved goodbye to Henry and Wexley in the training yard at Barkyard Boarding, a good session with the stubborn beagle doing little for his mood. Four days had passed since he'd shared his bed—briefly—with Bethany at his house, since their conversation about her leaving. Each night since, she came home on the late side with Meatball. The two of them would go for a walk, and then both disappeared into the guest room. She woke up early and left for work before he'd come downstairs, ruining his grand plan of winning her over with an elaborate breakfast menu.

As if French toast with powdered sugar and straw-berries would keep her in Spring Forest. In his life. If he and Wyatt couldn't accomplish that, comfort food certainly wouldn't.

She didn't want comfort. That was the problem. That was his mistake, thinking that the warm fuzzies of family life would get through, blast through the walls of her emotional defenses.

Bethany Robeson wasn't a puppy seeking a warm bed, loving arms and liver snaps. He understood that better now. She was more like a guarded stray, used to being on her own, fending for herself, not expect-ing anything soft or sweet. Not expecting *anything*.

How many guarded strays had he won over dur-ing the course of his career? A lot.

But Bethany was a human being, a woman, and her own person.

He was so tied up in knots that he was comparing the woman he loved—with all his heart—to canines.

He'd texted her every day, asking how she was, if everything was okay, and she'd text back a quick Everything's fine with a smiley face.

Everything wasn't fine, but she seemed to be working something out, and maybe he needed to give her the space to do that. He did have a busy life of his own. A baby. A business. His after-school ses-sions with Danny and Pickles twice a week, which were going great. His mother had been minding her own business the past few days too, which was always nice. And unexpected.

The problem was, he missed Bethany. Missed the intimacy. Missed getting to know her better and better every day. Missed helping her see that who she was, at heart, deep down, was for her to decide. Then again, part of the problem was that she *had* decided, and he was trying to get her to change the labels she'd stuck herself with.

Maybe he should let her be who she insisted she was. A woman alone, a lone wolf. No husband, no kids, no pets.

It just killed him to know that she was letting her past dictate her future. But he'd tried to change her mind, and he'd failed—his least favorite word.

The good news was that she was scheduled to bring in Meatball to Barkyard Boarding today to see if the basset hound might enjoy treadmill training and the "pre-beginner" agility course, starting slow and working his way up. So at least he'd see Bethany for forty-five minutes, get to talk to her in person.

Right on time, Bethany arrived with Meatball wearing the Adopt Me banner. Despite the pit in his stomach at how distant Bethany had been these past few days, he had to smile at Meatball. The heavy-set pup plodded along slowly, his long, droopy ears barely swaying.

"There's my buddy," Shane said, coming over to give Meatball a good rubbing. "Let's get this boy started."

She glanced at him and seemed about to say something, but followed him to the doggie treadmill area. Bethany took off the banner, unhooked the leash and encouraged Meatball up on the treadmill. He easily stepped on, but then stepped off.

Shane knelt beside him. "No?" he asked.

Meatball laid down, which was answer enough. He refused to look at the treadmill.

"Given his age and weight, I don't think we should push the treadmill if he's already showing he's not comfortable."

"Agreed," Bethany said. "Maybe just some light agility training instead?"

Shane nodded. "I'll start slow and walk him around the perimeter and see how he does. If he's moving at a good clip, we'll try an incline or two."

Bethany nodded.

"Haven't seen you much lately," Shane blurted out.

She glanced away for a moment. "I know. I'm sorry. There's a lot weighing on me. I had another conversation with your mom too."

He shook his head. "Is that why you've been avoiding me? I know we had a tough conversation ourselves, but what the hell did my mother say this time?"

"No—it's not like that," she said, touching his arm for a moment. "She was actually very honest. She apologized for interfering twelve years ago. It's clear she's not my biggest fan but that's fine. Not everyone is going to be. But she did say something really interesting—that Elliot didn't *know* if he was my father."

"Really?" he asked. "I guess he must have told her that."

"But if that's the case, why leave me the house? Why have the lawyer repeat his words—that he claims me as his daughter? It doesn't make sense." She let out a sigh. "I think your mom might know more than she's willing to say. Did she and Elliot become friendlier the past couple of years?"

He thought about that for a second. "Yes, friendlier is the right word. As I said, they were never really friends. No neighborly barbecues or anything like that. But they did talk sometimes. I came over for a visit about two months before he died and did see them sitting on the steps of Elliot's house. That was unusual."

"She knows something."

"I wouldn't get your hopes up about her sharing anything, Bethany—if she even has anything real to share. Maybe she got nosy and asked, and he told her he doesn't know because he doesn't want her to know anything."

"Maybe."

"Can I tell you something else? I think it's a good sign that you seem to want to know now—if he is your father."

Bethany bristled. "I'm still not sure I do."

"But you're asking questions. That means you're dealing with your past and facing hard things to think about, things that have been pressing on you since you were very little. This is the path that will lead you to closure. Peace."

She didn't look at all at peace.

"Excuse me," called a male voice.

They turned around. One of his groomer's clients was headed toward them.

"What a beautiful basset hound!" the man said. "Look at those eyes. Those ears!"

That got a smile out of Bethany.

"And he's working on his beer belly, huh?" the man continued. "What a trouper. He's a real beauty. I've always loved basset hounds. Is he yours?" he asked Bethany.

"No, I'm just fostering him. He'll be available for

adoption from Furever Paws once we get him down a few pounds and a bit out of his shell. He's nine years old and such a sweet, gentle dog."

"He's really great," the man said, his expression soft. "Those ears!" he said again.

Bethany laughed. "I know. I love petting them."

The man watched Meatball get his exercise in. "Well, it was great to meet you, Meatball." He turned to Bethany. "So I can put in an application for him to get the ball rolling?"

Shane could feel Bethany hesitate. Interesting.

"Of course!" she said. "Would you feel comfortable committing to his weight loss regimen? We're working hard on that."

"Well, I'd prefer to adopt him once he's closer to his goal weight. You think he'll be able to shed the pounds? He is a bit…rotund."

"Enough to pass our veterinarian's health check," Bethany said.

"I'll be in touch, then. You just might see an application from me."

"Great," Bethany said. "Nice to meet you."

They watched the man walk away. When he disappeared through the doors, Bethany crossed her arms over her chest. "I don't know. He seemed really interested at first but maybe only if Meatball successfully loses the weight."

"That's for Meatball's own good anyway," Shane said. "He seemed like a nice guy."

Bethany let out a sigh. Her third since arriving. "He did seem nice."

"I can't imagine you giving Meatball up," Shane said. "You love that dog."

Her beautiful green eyes looked so sad he wanted to wrap his arms around her. "I've had to give up those I've loved before. Remember?" Before he could say a word, she added, "Would you mind dropping Meatball off at the shelter after he's done?"

"Bethany, don't run away."

"I've just got to get back to work. And to be honest, yes, I'm sadder than I thought I'd be about someone adopting Meatball. I did let myself get attached—to Meatball…and to you. But that was a mistake when I know I'm going to have to let you both go."

She practically ran out the door.

He understood—she very likely felt that everything was closing in on her. Meatball possibly getting adopted. She was on the verge of learning the truth about who her father was. And her up and down relationship with Shane had her in turmoil, too.

Her hand was being forced and she'd either confront everything and let herself finally deal with it all—or she'd run.

Shane was very afraid she was going to run.

He looked at Meatball, tail wagging, but he felt anything but happy himself. He'd done what he promised he wouldn't. He'd let himself get all distracted, all torn up, over his feelings for Bethany—who'd always said she was leaving.

It was time to back off. Put some space and distance between them.

For Wyatt's sake. And for his.

His phone pinged with a text. From Grant.

Up for a quick, casual dinner tonight at our place before we have to get the babies to sleep? Plus we have a question for you.

Perfect. The focus would be on the babies, as it was whenever he and the Whitakers got together—going over schedules, trading sweet stories and nightmarish times, laughing at how funny their babies were.

He needed more of this. Baby-focused time. Not love-life focused.

I'll be there, he typed back.

Bethany looked at herself in the bathroom mirror at Furever Paws, making sure she didn't have dog food on her shirt or cat hair all over her. No to the dog food, yes to the cat hair. She'd brushed a few of the cats that morning—and then had spent the past hour with the four German shepherds, playing with them in the yard, working on their trust level, just trying to let them have some old-fashioned fun. They loved chasing balls and sticks and dropping them at her feet, waiting patiently for her to throw again. That they could run so well was a great indicator of how fast their health was improving.

She grabbed the jumbo-sized lint roller and gave herself a sweep. Rebekah had invited her over for a quick, casual dinner, and it was just what Bethany needed. Girl talk. She assumed Grant and the twins would be out since Rebekah hadn't mentioned them in her text.

She went back into her office to say goodbye to Meatball. "I'll be back for you after dinner at Rebekah's. Then we'll go to Shane's as usual." She didn't want to drop him off at Shane's beforehand since things were a bit…strained between them.

She knelt down, her heart suddenly clenching at the idea of soon saying goodbye to this sweet, beautiful creature who'd kept her such good company since she'd arrived. She'd met him her very first day back in town. She buried her face in his side and gave him a good rub, then stood up and realized she was covered in dog hair again. Oh well, such was life at an animal rescue. Rebekah wouldn't hold it against her.

She gave herself another quick swipe with the lint

roller, then headed out to the Whitakers. She slowed as she turned onto their street, looking for the "red brick" house. But her heart rate sped up as she noticed the truck in the driveway.

Barkyard Boarding.

Shane was here?

She parked beside his truck and then headed to the front door with the raspberry cheesecake she'd stopped at the bakery for, clearing her throat as she rang the doorbell.

Rebekah answered the door with Lily in her arms.

"Well, hello there, cutie," Bethany said to the baby. *Please don't get all fussy at the sight of me. Pleeeeze.*

Thankfully, the beautiful baby girl just stared at her.

Now that she was safe on the fussy baby front, she moved on to the even scarier possibility. "Shane's here?" Bethany blurted out.

Rebekah slapped her palm to her forehead with her free hand. "Did I not say that in my text? This is exactly what I mean by being spread too thin—I totally forgot to mention that we invited *both* of you as a thanks for watching the twins last week."

Oh boy.

She followed Rebekah into the dining room, where Shane and Grant both stood and greeted her,

Shane looking surprised to see her. And gorgeous. And sexy. Wyatt was asleep in a swing in the corner, as was Lucas. Lily let out a big yawn, and Rebekah gave her a kiss on the head and placed her in the double swing beside her twin, light lullabies drifting from the speaker.

"I didn't know you were coming," Shane said. Awkwardly. "I would have offered to drive."

Hmm. Were Grant and Rebekah doing a little matchmaking? "I came straight from the rescue. No worries."

Grant sat down. Tall and handsome, he had slightly dark circles under his eyes. "Just when both babies started to sleep through the night, they also started teething, so the 3:00 a.m. shrieking wake-ups have turned us into zombies." He jerked his torso a few times and made his expression blank, his head hanging to the left.

Shane laughed. "Oh, I know all about that." He sat too.

Rebekah took the chair beside him and gave him something of a smile, which he returned.

This was definitely a little awkward.

"Dig in to the taco bar," Rebekah said, waving her hand at the assortment of fixings in the center of the table.

There were hard and soft shells, fragrant ground

beef, black beans, cheese, shredded lettuce, jalapeños, which Bethany would skip, sour cream and a
few different kinds of salsa. Bethany loved tacos.

She took a bite of her stuffed hard-shell taco, lots
of crunching going on at the table.

"Mmm, delicious," she said.

"Something tells me these three," Shane said
pointing at the sleeping trio, "are going to be taco
junkies by age three. Not that that's a bad thing. I
could live on tacos."

"Same," Grant said. "With extra jalapeños." He
popped up and started pouring their drinks from a
pitcher into their fancy cocktail glasses. "Virgin frozen margaritas. To help us stay awake for the teething shrieks."

By the time she was halfway through her first
taco, Bethany had relaxed. The company was fun
and the conversation fast-moving, so there were no
awkward silences.

"You said you had a question for me," Shane asked
Grant, building his second taco.

"Oh, that's right," Grant said. "Like I said, my
mind is not my own, so I'm glad you reminded me.
I'm pretty sure I remember you mentioning you had
a friend who has a horse farm? A breeder, maybe?
We're thinking of surprising my sister Josie with

horseback riding lessons for her birthday. She's always wanted to take lessons."

Rebekah nodded. "Now that Josie's daughter confirmed she's not coming home for spring break, we figured a special kind of gift, an experience gift, would be nice for her."

"What a great idea," Bethany said with a nod. "And so thoughtful. I've gotten to know Josie a little, and I'll bet she'd love that."

And yeah, maybe it would give Josie something wonderful to look forward to since she wouldn't be seeing her daughter until summer, most likely. This was just what happened in life—children grew up and sometimes moved far away for school or a new adventure. People left—they broke your heart even if they didn't mean to, like Josie's daughter.

Another reinforcement for Bethany to keep her head on straight about what she was doing in Spring Forest, to stick to her plans.

"Declan Hoyt," Shane said, grabbing another taco shell. "He's a horse breeder who has stables just outside Spring Forest. He's your guy."

Grant pulled out his phone, adding a note and the name. "Thanks."

"I'm pretty sure his teenage niece recently moved in or is moving in soon," Shane added. "Some family issues there, I think. So I'm not sure how much time he'll have for riding lessons, but definitely get in touch."

"We will," Rebekah said. "And hey, if anyone knows teens, it's Josie."

Bethany glanced at Shane. The camaraderie and conversation had eased the tension between them. That would make tonight less awkward.

You could always sleep on the cot at the shelter, she reminded herself. *You don't* have *to stay with Shane.*

Which was how she knew she wanted to, despite everything.

Chapter Seventeen

Bethany woke up the next morning in Shane's guest room, her mind as cluttered and unsettled as it had been all night while she tossed and turned. The thing that was really bothering her was that she wasn't the *only* one in the house trying to keep her distance. She could tell that Shane was too. Emotionally and physically. He'd been friendly enough at dinner with the Whitakers, and they'd left separately, since they'd arrived that way, and she had to pick up Meatball from Furever Paws and check in with the overnight staff.

When she'd gotten to Shane's house with Meatball, who'd seemed a bit more subdued than usual, the dog stretched out on the kitchen rug while Bethany made herself a cup of tea. She'd offered to make Shane a cup, but he'd declined and didn't join her at the kitchen table. He hadn't hung out with her in the backyard when she took Meatball outside for a bit.

And there was certainly no intense kiss that would lead her and Shane right back into bed. It seemed that Shane had heard her loud and clear and respected her feelings.

For the best, she thought, all too aware her heart had plummeted two notches.

She forced herself out of the comfortable bed and walked over to where Meatball lay in a strange position across the rug. Huh. Not curled up in his plush dog bed as usual. He lay stretched out, as he'd been briefly last night in the kitchen, and he didn't lift his head when Bethany sat down beside him.

"Meatball?" she said, looking him over. "You okay?" His eyes appeared a bit cloudy, a bit sunken underneath. And his belly appeared bloated, in a way that didn't correspond to his extra weight.

No head lift. No tail wag. He just lay there. Seeming...unwell.

"Shane?" she called out.

No response.

She hurried out but his room was empty. She found him downstairs in the kitchen, taking Wyatt from his chair and placing him in the baby swing.

"I think something's wrong with Meatball," she said in a rush of words. "I've never seen him like this."

They hadn't changed his food at Furever Paws, and he'd only done some walking yesterday at Barkyard Boarding since he'd shown no interest in the treadmill.

Shane shot her a worried gaze, then took the stairs two a time, Bethany right behind him. He kneeled beside the dog, very gently touching Meatball's belly. The dog winced and let out a high-pitched yip. Very un-Meatball-like. Something was definitely wrong.

"Let's get him to Doc J right away. Hang on—I'll be right back." He rushed out, then returned in thirty seconds carrying what looked like a stretcher. "I'll get him on here and then we'll very carefully bring him down the stairs and slide this into the kennel in my truck."

"Okay," she said, dread filling her chest. Everything was going to be okay, she told herself. Meatball was going to be okay. Dogs got sick sometimes. He'd pull through. He *had* to.

Shane gently wedged the stretcher under Meatball and they both took an end, Shane walking backward. Meatball definitely wasn't doing well because he barely seemed to notice he was moving in the air. They got him down the stairs and into the truck.

"I'll go get Wyatt, and then we're off," he said. He

was back in a minute with the baby in his carrier and his bag. After buckling Wyatt in his car seat, they headed toward town.

"He's got to be okay," she said. "Hear that, Meatball," she called out. "You've got to be okay because someone is interesting in adopting you. You want your 'furever' home, don't you?"

Though she was trying so hard to sound light and optimistic, as soon as those words came out, she burst into tears, sitting there shaking as tears ran down her cheeks.

Shane took her hand with his free one. "Doc J will take care of him. No worrying till we have to, okay?"

She knew he was right, and yet the tears just wouldn't stop.

Shane pulled into the parking lot and grabbed his phone. "I just texted Doc J and Birdie that Meatball is very ill, that it might be bloat, and that we're here at the clinic." His phone pinged. "Doc J says he and Birdie will be here in thirty seconds." Luckily, the Whitaker farmhouse was right on the property.

"Okay," she said, trying to breathe. She swiped under her eyes. "Doc J is the best. He'll take good care of Meatball." No sooner had she said his name than the tears started falling again.

"I'll bring in Wyatt and get him settled behind

the front desk, then I'll come right back and we'll bring Meatball in."

She nodded, unable to speak.

Shane quickly took out Wyatt's car seat and disappeared inside Furever Paws, then ran back out. Bethany could see Maya at the front desk, picking Wyatt up and holding him on her lap. She was so grateful for these wonderful people around her who always rushed to help.

She and Shane had just gotten Meatball onto the exam table in the clinic when Birdie and Doc J came rushing in, him washing his hands at the sink, Birdie very clearly concerned as she looked over Meatball lying there looking completely miserable. One of Doc J's vet techs arrived, her gaze soft on the basset hound on the table.

"Okay, you two wait outside, please," Doc J said, looking from Shane to Bethany. "I'll come get you the moment I finish the exam."

Bethany nodded, glanced at Shane, and they left the exam room. "He has to be okay. Has to be. If I say it enough times, it'll be true, right? I think it's stomach related. Maybe torsion?" she asked, thinking about how painful that twisted stomach condition could be. If you didn't treat it fast enough, it could be fatal. "Doc J can treat him since we got him here fast, right?"

"I was thinking torsion too. I think he's going to be okay, Bethany. Like you said, Doc J is the best. Plus he loves Meatball just like we do."

I do love Meatball, she thought, tears pricking her eyes again. *I love that dog. So damned much.*

I'm not supposed to love the dogs I foster. That's how I'm able to give them up when a good forever home comes their way. You're not supposed to fall in love. With anything or anyone.

Bethany ran outside and stopped in front of the Furever Paws logo on the building, the cat and dog silhouetted in a heart. She couldn't gulp in fresh air fast enough.

Shane was beside her in two seconds, pulling her into his arms and wrapping her in a hug she desperately needed. "He's in good hands."

She let herself relax against him, so comforted by his strong arms and hands, the wall of his chest, his head resting atop hers. She could stay here forever. Right now, with Shane's arms around her, she could almost believe things would be okay.

"Let's go hang out in the dog room with the German shepherds," Shane said, his hand gentle under her chin. "They were in very sorry shape when they came in and they're getting healthier and stronger every day. Seeing them will lift your spirits and give you hope."

They certainly had last night before she'd gone to the Whitakers. "Okay," she said. She meant to turn to go in, but instead wrapped her arms tightly around him. "Thank you, Shane," she said, looking up at him. "You're always there for me. Always have the right words. I don't know how you do it, but you do."

He tightened his hold on her, and again the comfort was so necessary she didn't want to move. But he took her hand and led her inside. He stopped at the front desk to take Wyatt from Maya, who made a sad face at having to let him go, and Shane thanked her for watching him.

The four German shepherds were in the dog run with two of the volunteers. Bethany and Shane stood between the double gates, watching them.

"See those German shepherds, Wyatt?" Shane asked, pointing as he hoisted the baby in his arms. "They're beautiful, majestic dogs."

Bethany gave a nod. They were indeed. Sweet Jedidiah, who'd been the most ill, was looking so much better and had definitely filled out, though he still hadn't fully recovered. Bethany smiled at him, thinking about how Wendy Alvarez from Pets for Vets would be coming in a couple of weeks to assess the shepherds as possible service dogs for veterans. Jethro, Jester and Joshua were playing with their favorite toys in the cool morning sunshine. Any time the volunteers threw a ball, the four shepherds would go running for it. The sight of them—strong, happy, running free in the yard and playing—did wonders for Bethany's soul at the moment.

Her phone chimed with a text, and Bethany jumped, her heart suddenly pounding.

It was from Doc J. Have a diagnosis. He's going into surgery and I think he'll pull through fine. Come on in. I have a few minutes to talk.

Bethany held up her phone. "Surgery. I hope he's going to be okay."

"Let's go to talk to him," Shane said, and they headed back inside. Maya was very happy to take back the baby for a little while.

In the exam room inside the clinic, Meatball was being prepped for surgery, and Bethany's heart lurched. Seeing him lying there, sedated, tubes and wires… It was almost too much. And she'd seen this countless times. She'd met with veterinarians in exam rooms with dogs in all kinds of condition— with every possible ailment.

Meatball has your heart in a way you didn't think would be possible. That's why you're so affected.

"Torsion," Doc J said. "I imagine you probably suspected it yourselves. Common but dangerous. The stomach twists and I need to go in and get it right again. It's surgery so it comes with risks. But I'm hopeful that Meatball will be just fine."

Bethany bit her lip. She felt Shane move behind her and place his strong, warm hands on her shoulders. Just as she'd said before, he was always there. "I'll stay with him tonight as he's recuperating."

"Me too," Shane said.

She wasn't going to turn that down. She needed Shane right now—and she'd need him tonight.

"Think positively," Birdie said, nodding at Bethany. "I know it's scary. But he's in the best possible hands. I'll be in my office during the surgery, so come hang out if you need a shoulder and tissues, okay?"

"I will," she said. She turned to Doc J. "Thank you. I know you'll do everything you can for him."

The room got busy, Meatball being wheeled away into the surgical room two doors down, fully equipped thanks to Grant Whitaker's financial ingenuity and the generosity of the town and entire county.

Suddenly it was just the two of them again.

"Call me if there's any news," Shane said. "I need to get Wyatt to his mom's, and then I have a few hours to put in at Barkyard Boarding. But I *am* keeping you company here tonight. We don't have to talk. I'm just going to be here for you."

It was exactly what she needed. That much she knew for sure. "I appreciate it."

He nodded, kissed her on the top of her head and then left.

She missed him the moment he was through the door.

Chapter Eighteen

At six thirty that night, Shane moved the cot from the vacant office into the recuperation room, which Meatball had to himself tonight. Well, except for two worried humans. The surgery had been a success, but the danger wasn't over yet. He was weak and a senior, and everything depended on how he did through the night.

Shane spread his sleeping bag on the other side of the room so that when Bethany returned from getting takeout for them, she wouldn't think he was trying to sleep in touching distance. He needed to give her space and hold her tight at the same time. Not an easy balance to maintain. But so far, he seemed to be doing what she needed.

For some reason, it came naturally.

No—he actually knew the reason. Because he cared about her so much that he thought his heart would burst with it.

He was about to reach for his water bottle in his backpack when he thought he heard the sound of crying. A child. He poked his head out into the hallway.

A woman and child who he recognized from around town—Renee Hobbs and her daughter, Brooklyn, who couldn't be more than eight or nine—stood staring into the large viewing window to the cat room. Bethany was beside them, holding the take-out bag from the Main Street Grill. Brooklyn was crying. Her mother looked worried. So did Bethany.

"He's definitely not in there," Brooklyn said as she looked through the glass, her face crumpling. "I see a few orange cats but none of them are Oliver. I was hoping someone found him and brought him here."

Oh dammit, he thought, suddenly understanding what was going on. A lost pet.

"If someone does bring him here, I'll call you right away," Bethany said. "You have my promise, Brooklyn."

"It's all my fault," the girl said, sobbing. "I accidentally left the door open a couple days ago and Oliver got out. He hasn't come home and no one has seen him." She covered her face with her hands, her thin shoulders shaking.

Her mom pulled her into a hug. "Hey," she said soothingly. "Oliver will either come home or he'll be found. Everyone in this town really cares about animals. We put up Missing Cat flyers all over Spring Forest. It has all our information. Someone will find him and call us, okay, honey?"

Brooklyn sobbed harder.

"Your mom's right, Brooklyn," Bethany said. "It might not be right away, but there will be a lot of people keeping an eye out for Oliver. I'll personally look for him too, okay? I know it's really hard, but try to think positive thoughts."

He could see Bethany freeze for a second, as if she was letting her own words, her own very good advice, sink in to herself.

Yes, he thought.

She turned to Renee. "Do you have a flyer with you? I'll put it on our bulletin board."

Renee nodded and pulled out the flyer from her tote bag and handed it to Bethany.

He walked toward them. "Hi, I'm Shane from Barkyard Boarding. I'll look for Oliver too. I'll post your flyer at my business."

"We appreciate that," Renee said, her eyes teary as she gave Shane a flyer too.

They walked the Hobbs family to the lobby, Maya posting the flyer with Oliver's photo and contact information on the bulletin board.

As they headed back to the recuperation room, Bethany looked absolutely miserable. She put the take-out bag on the small round table by the door. "I got chicken soup for myself," she said. "I'm sure I won't be able to eat more than a few spoonfuls."

They both sat down, glancing at Meatball in the large, padded kennel, his eyes closed.

"At least it's something," he said. "And comfort food."

She nodded, handing him his circular container with his BLT and fries, but he too had little appetite.

"I know that cats can return even weeks later, so I won't give up hope for the Hobbs family," she said. "But it's a solid reminder that things go wrong. Dogs get sick and may not pull through the night. Cats run away, making small children sob. And everything in life just breaks your damned heart."

He knew all about broken hearts. "There's a flip side to all that, though. You might get hurt when you open your heart, but you also get the beautiful, happy times. You can't miss something you didn't love in the first place. *Loving* is worth it, Bethany.

You know that phrase, that it's better to have loved and lost than never to have loved at all."

"Is it?" she asked, looking at him, her beautiful green eyes so sad and worried.

He wanted to touch her face, to hold her close, but he kept his hands to himself. "Damned straight, it is."

"I don't know, Shane," she whispered. "I really don't."

He knew. But that wasn't going to get her to stay.

He'd tried so hard to break through, but he had to prepare himself for the idea that she was going to walk—no, run—right out of his life. Again.

The entire staff, even those who hadn't worked today, stopped by to ask after Meatball and bring him a gift. *Everyone.* Bethany had been surprised by the first worker who'd shown up on his own time, squeaky toy in hand, and she'd been sobbing by the tenth, who'd arrived with tears in her eyes and a little bag of low-calorie liver snaps. The kindness, the compassion—she'd been blown away.

Birdie and Doc J had bought Meatball a new bed, bigger and with special orthopedic technology she couldn't even pronounce. Shane, no surprise, had bought a very soft fleece blanket from the Furever Paws gift shop when he'd arrived back at the shelter.

She was surrounded by kindness. She'd never forget it. No matter where she ended up.

Now, close to midnight, it was just Bethany and Shane at the rescue. One would always stay with Meatball in the recuperation room, and the other would check on the shepherds and the other animals. Bethany had gone to the dog room to let herself cry over Meatball since she didn't want to break down in front of Shane again. Plus she'd needed a little space from being so close to him, the gorgeous, sexy, wonderful man who had turned her entire life around and created options she'd never expected to be on the table.

Shane. Wyatt. Spring Forest. A life here.

Or the lack of risk back home in Berryville where she'd find a space for a new pet rescue center. Where she could devote herself to dogs and cats and rabbits and birds and furry rodents who needed homes and would find them.

No husband, no kids, no pets. A life without loss.

What do you call this? she asked herself, picturing Meatball in his recuperation kennel under sedation. He might not make it through the night. Loss with a capital *L*.

And what do you call leaving Furever Paws, and Meatball?

Leaving Shane and Wyatt and Spring Forest?

Loss.

She closed her eyes, watching the shepherds sleep, one occasionally opening his eyes to peer at her. *I'm here*, she'd whisper, and the eyes would close again. Assured, comforted by her presence.

Each time, her heart would clench and shutter. She was feeling way too much.

Better to have loved and lost...

Was it?

She got up and headed back to the recuperation room. Shane was sitting in front of Meatball's cage, his knees up to his chest, watching the basset hound sleep. He loved Meatball too, she knew.

"The shepherds are asleep," she said, and he stood up, now way too close, even though he was several feet away. All that height, those muscles, his face, the sexy light brown hair, the blue eyes that were so hard to look away from.

"Good. Meatball's breathing well. That's a good sign, Bethany. No ragged breathing, like Doc J said to watch for."

She nodded, her gaze now on the dog. *Please make it through, Meatball*, she prayed. *Please*.

"Bethany, I know you've got a lot to think about. Or maybe you've made up your mind and you're leaving and that's it. But no matter what, just know that tonight, I'm your friend and I'm here for you.

You need a hug, I've got these," he added, holding out his arms.

She burst into tears again and walked into his body, letting herself be wrapped in his warm, strong, comforting embrace. "I'm so scared." She let out a breath. "He's just so special."

Like you.

"Whatever you need from me tonight, Bethany. Take it. It's yours. Okay? No questions asked. No expectations."

She looked up at him. "Can I share your sleeping bag?"

"Of course."

So they slid inside, both fully dressed, Bethany spooned against his long, muscular body, his arm around her torso, his hand smoothing her hair. They laid like that for hours, Shane insisting on being the one who stayed awake to watch for any signs of distress from Meatball, and anytime she opened her eyes, he would squeeze her hand or run his hand through her hair, letting her know he'd kept his promise to keep vigil. Over both her and Meatball.

How did anyone, even someone so self-protectively solitary, walk away from this kind of…care? What kind of person would reject this?

Someone who knew it was as temporary as everything always was. The safety of that, of knowing her limitations, allowed her to drift off.

The morning sun coming through the white blinds woke Bethany up. Shane was beside her, looking exhausted and somehow still gorgeous.

She slid out of the sleeping bag and went over to Meatball's kennel. His eyes slightly opened and he looked at her, and she smiled. "You're okay, Meatball. You made it through."

"He did," Shane said. "Doc J and Birdie will be here at six thirty. I'll go get us some coffee."

He came back with two mugs. "There's also the quiche and doughnuts Josie dropped off last night," he said. "But I'm out of hands."

"I don't think I can eat a bite until Doc J says Meatball is okay."

"Me too," Shane said.

She sipped her coffee, cream, one sugar, just the way she liked it. Of course.

Fifteen minutes later, Doc J and Birdie came in. After an exam, he gave Bethany and Shane the good news they'd been waiting for.

Meatball was going to be okay.

Bethany's knees shook to the point that Shane had to take her mug so she wouldn't spill coffee all over herself. She thanked Doc J profusely, and there were many hugs, and then it was just her and Shane again.

"Adopt him," Shane said. "Adopt Meatball."

Bethany stared at him. "What? You know I can't do that."

"Why not? He's your dog. He's the dog of your life, Bethany. You *love* him. You could have lost him but you didn't. Now you can adopt him."

She slowly shook her head. "You know how I feel about that. I…" She trailed off, her head feeling like it was stuffed with rags. "Shane, stop it."

"Yes, I'm pushing, Bethany. But you need a push. You need someone to tell you that you can come home. That you *are* home. That Meatball is your dog."

Tears pricked her eyes. Her phone pinged. A reason to turn away. She looked at the screen. "It's Harris. The house is done. I can come see it this morning."

That means it's time to leave, she thought, her heart racing, chills running up her spine.

"Bethany."

"I need to go," she said. "I'm sorry, Shane. I'm sorry that I'm so…"

"Unwilling to let yourself be loved?"

She stared at him, then ran out. Very well aware she'd left her heart in that room.

Chapter Nineteen

As Bethany stood in the center of Elliot Bradley's house—her house—she still couldn't believe what Harris and his team had managed to accomplish in such a short amount of time. The kitchen was now modern, the bathrooms updated, the walls painted a soothing off-white. The furniture had been sold or donated, including the his-and-her recliners, which had gone to a lovely senior couple who'd adopted two cats recently. Any number of people would come in for the open house and bid immediately, given the house's good location on a pretty street near the center of town.

She walked over to the big window in the living

room, looking out at the lawn that was coming in nicely, the first spring flowers just poking through.

She almost jumped.

Standing there, scowling at her as she exited her car was Anna Dupree, carrying Princess.

Bethany wouldn't mention the scary neighbor next door to the Realtor she planned to meet with today.

The sight of Shane's mother helped cement her resolve to get the place listed and sold as quickly as possible. And then she could leave.

As she'd done once before.

She lifted her chin and stepped out, needing to get back to Furever Paws.

"I ran into Harris Vega this morning," Anna called over. "He said the house is finished. I guess you'll be leaving town soon."

"I'm sure that makes you very happy," Bethany called back. She'd had it with trying to be pleasant to this woman.

Except Anna didn't call back a yes. Or gloat.

She burst into tears, causing a confused Princess to tilt her head and lick Anna's face.

This was unexpected.

Bethany sucked in a breath and walked over to the woman. "Can I help?"

Anna shifted the Chihuahua in her arms to free a hand to wipe under her eyes. "The last time I saw

Shane really, truly happy was before you left twelve years ago. Before everything blew up. I didn't know how bad things were about to get. I didn't know that all his plans were going to disintegrate. And I certainly didn't know how much he loved you." She stared down at the ground for a moment. "I don't think he'll ever forgive me for what I did, and I don't know how to change things between us."

"I shouldn't speak for Shane, but I think he just wants you on his side," Bethany said.

She tilted her head like Princess had. "Is it that simple?"

Bethany gave something of a smile. "Actually, yes. But not just once, not to get back in his good graces. *All* the time. You can disagree with his choices, but be supportive, regardless. That's how you show respect."

Anna seemed to be taking that all in, mulling it over, her blue eyes working, thinking. Then she glanced up at the white colonial, clearly needing to change the subject. "Are you leaving town like everyone says you are now that the house is ready to be listed?"

She'd stopped at Shane's on the way here to pack her bag. She could leave right now.

Not that she would. She was hardly ready to say goodbye to Meatball. To say goodbye to Furever

Paws and Birdie and Rebekah and Josie and the amazing staff and volunteers.

To say goodbye to Shane. And Wyatt.

Her heart clenched.

"Are people really still talking about me?" Bethany shook her head.

"Not in a bad way. Not in a gossipy way like before."

Bethany raised an eyebrow. "I guess that's something. And yes, I am leaving. That was always my plan. Some people are meant for—" What was she doing? Just stop talking, Bethany. Wasn't this Shane's evil mother, for Pete's sake?

"Some people are meant for what?" Anna asked.

"Marriage. Kids. A dog." Now tears pricked her eyes, and she blinked them back hard. "But I'm not one of those people. I'll always be Kate Robeson's daughter, self-taught not to bother with all that. I'll always be the girl who doesn't know who her father is. I'll always be the girl you ran out of town."

Anna grimaced. "I treated you terribly back then. And without knowing it, I treated Shane terribly in the process. I'm very sorry, Bethany. And I have news for you—you're not that girl. I mean, maybe deep down you'll always remember that girl, but you're your own woman. I think you are, anyway. I don't really know you. You just seem like a good person, kind, smart. You run that animal shelter, so Birdie Whitaker must think well of you. I got Princess from there years ago."

Bethany smiled and reached out a hand to the Chihuahua. "I really didn't expect the conversation to go like this."

"Maybe it's proof that things—and people—can change," Anna said. "I don't like change, never have."

"It's all I ever wanted," Bethany said. "And now that I have it in spades, a whole different path right in front of me, I'm running away from it. Back to what I know. Being alone. No husband, no kids, no pets." She stared down at her feet.

"Elliot buried documentation about your paternity in his backyard."

Bethany's head snapped up. "What?"

Anna nodded.

Bethany stared at her, barely able to process what she'd just heard. "He had documentation? I *am* his daughter?"

"I'll tell you everything he told me—just a few months ago. He never did find out if you were or not, even though he had the results of the DNA test."

"But how—"

Anna held up a hand. "When you were very little, not even two years old, your mother took swabs of your cheek, but Elliot had been afraid to know whether he was your father or not, so she gave him the kit and said if he was ever ready to find out… He kept the kit in a safe in his office. And then a few months ago, he decided to find out once and for all. He was very down about how he'd lived his life and he said it was time."

Bethany gasped. "So he got a DNA kit of his own and he sent both in to test for paternity?"

Anna nodded. "I saw him sitting by that maple in the backyard, just sobbing. And I asked what was wrong, and he just let loose. Told me everything. He got the documentation, but he hadn't opened the envelope. He said he didn't want to know because what if you weren't his daughter? He said he wanted you to be. Even if he didn't deserve to be your dad. Said he was going to leave you the house and claim you as his regardless."

Bethany's mouth had dropped open a full minute ago. She sat down hard on the top step. "That's a lot to process." She looked up at Anna and stood, then threw her arms around the woman and Chihuahua. "Thank you for telling me. You didn't have to."

Anna hugged her back. Not with gusto, admittedly, but a hug nonetheless. "But you still don't know if he's your dad. I'm not sure telling you changes anything."

"Oh, it does," she said. "I have some thinking to do, but something feels very different."

Anna bit her lip. "It used to bother me the way your mother and Elliot loved each other so much. He'd promised his wife he'd never leave her and he didn't, and why *either* woman stuck around I don't know, but both made their choice, I suppose."

Bethany nodded. She could barely keep up with everything Anna was saying.

"I hated that I was jealous of a woman carrying on a torrid long-term affair with a married man," Anna continued. "Jealous of how much they loved each other. I'd see them sometimes around town, so wrapped up in each other that they didn't even notice I was there. I never had a love like that," Anna went on. "Not even when Shane's dad and I first married. The past year or so, Elliot was so alone. We started talking more, and he told me what Kate had meant to him." She threw up a hand. "I don't know what I'm saying. Adultery makes me sick. But life isn't so black and white, I suppose. I don't know." She nuzzled the little dog close.

"He didn't go to my mom's funeral, though," Bethany said. "I thought that had to mean he wasn't my father."

"He didn't go because he didn't feel it was his

place," Anna said. "He believed he'd failed Kate. He was there in his heart, though. I know that."

Black and white. Shades of gray.

Bethany had never been a believer in shades of gray. Adultery made her sick too. But it was time to let the past go. She understood that now.

"So the documentation is buried in a box beside that maple tree in the backyard?" Bethany asked.

Anna nodded. "Along with photos of your mother and letters she'd written to him over the years. Are you going to dig it up?"

"I don't know," she said.

Bethany didn't know anything right now. But she knew something inside her had changed.

Shane was still in a state of disbelief over the conversation he'd just had with his mother. She'd come to Barkyard Boarding a half hour ago and asked to talk to him, and he'd braced himself for another crappy conversation.

But she'd surprised him. Shocked him. Anna Dupree had opened up about her own past and apologized profusely for interfering in his life. They'd talked about his father, almost bringing Shane to tears. Then she'd said she'd had a long conversation with Bethany this morning. She hadn't gone into detail, saying that she didn't want to share Bethany's business, that it was up to Bethany, but she did confirm that they'd cleared the air.

Funny, his mother had said, if Bethany did stay in town, she could see them even being friends. She was actually thinking about volunteering at Furever Paws herself.

He'd gaped at her, then actually gave himself a little pinch on his forearm, which earned him a light smack on his biceps from his mother.

He and his mother had hugged for the first time in a long time. A real hug. When she'd left, he was rendered speechless for a good minute.

People could always surprise you.

So maybe Bethany would surprise him too.

He thought about what his mother had said about "Bethany's business." Maybe Anna really did know something about Elliot and whether he was Bethany's father and had told her.

If she wants to share it with you, she will, he told himself.

She doesn't want to share her life *with you, though. You have to be ready to let her go.*

But he wasn't. That much he knew for sure.

Bethany wouldn't leave without saying goodbye. Not like last time, where he got a very quick phone call. She'd come see him in person.

And he'd fight like hell one more time for her.

Because he loved her. He loved her with everything he had. And he had room in his heart to be Wyatt's dad and Bethany's guy. Each part of him made the other part stronger.

He hoped to have the chance to tell her that, to explain it. But would she hear him? Would he finally break through?

His love for her had smashed through his own defenses, but he'd been ready for Bethany Robeson all along. Waiting for her all these years, all this time. He just hadn't known it.

Bethany *hadn't* been ready for him. She'd been steamrolled, clobbered with him and his baby son. With a dog named Meatball. With a possible future she was too scared to think could be the real deal.

He understood. And he was going to fight for her.

His phone pinged with a text.

Birdie.

A Phillip Hartman filled out an application to adopt Meatball and put you down as a reference, says he's a client of yours. I'll leave you to talk to Bethany about this.

Shane froze. So Phillip had gotten the ball rolling as he said he might. This was the first application Meatball had gotten—ever. That beautiful dog had languished at Furever Paws for months. Shane shook his head as he thought of that sweet, soulful basset hound and all the poor guy—who had a lot of life left in him—had gone through. Meatball deserved the best.

His phone pinged again.

Oh, Birdie added, the guy wants to know if Meatball lost any of his beer belly.

Shane sighed. Some people wanted a perfect dog. Well, Meatball had just come through a really hard night. His beer belly could wait a bit.

I'll talk to Bethany, he texted back.

He sucked in a breath. No way would she let Meatball go. It would be a solid week before Doc J would clear him for adoption, but he didn't believe Bethany would really let the dog of her heart go to someone else.

She's planning to let you go, he thought. *You and Wyatt*. No, he thought. No way. The woman he'd come to know wouldn't leave them all behind.

He texted Bethany. That guy we met at Barkyard who liked Meatball—he put in an application. You'll have to do a home check and all that but Meatball finally has a chance at a forever home.

There was a flurry of dots indicating that she was texting back.

But then they disappeared. Then started again. Stopped.

Started again. Stopped.

This was what we all wanted, right? she finally texted.

He felt his heart crack in a terrible zigzag.

Maybe so, he texted back. But it's not what I hoped you'd say. Because if you could adopt Meatball yourself, you could join a family of two and bring two to the party—yourself and Meatball. You'd both be in your forever home.

No ellipses indicating that she was typing. Nothing. Radio silence.

Bethany didn't really have the money for a motel room but she needed some space tonight—to think, to be in Spring Forest without all the reminders of what would keep her here. So she'd texted Birdie that she needed to take the rest of the day off—Birdie had been very understanding—and booked herself a room at the Dogwood Bed & Breakfast on Second Street, which was parallel to Main Street. Not very far from Barkyard Boarding.

Of course, the B&B *had* to have the word *dog* in its name and remind Bethany of Meatball, not that she could stop thinking about him. Dogwood was the state flower of North Carolina and there had been a sweet bouquet of the white blooms waiting for her in her room.

Now she sat on the back porch with a cup of herbal tea and one of the proprietor's delicious mixed-berry scones. But she had no appetite. The tea had gone cold and the scone remained untouched. The news about Meatball's application on top of all Shane's mother had told her had overwhelmed her to the point that she'd almost sunk to her knees.

For the past few hours she'd thought nonstop about what she'd learned from Anna. How Elliot hadn't wanted to know that Bethany *wasn't* his daughter, so he'd buried the results of the paternity test without opening it. How he'd left her the house, claiming her as his child because he *wanted* her to be.

Something in that had gotten to Bethany, started knocking at the brick wall that had surrounded her heart.

Elliot had chosen *his* truth instead of having the choice made for him in black and white.

Black and white. Shades of gray.

She looked up at the sky, the sun just beginning to set over Spring Forest. *I don't fully understand you, Mom, and I probably never will. But I don't have to in order to love you. I always loved you and I always will.*

Tears pricked her eyes and again she felt something shift in her chest, another piece of the brick wall crumbling.

She tried to blink away the tears as she pictured Meatball in his padded recuperation kennel, his long silky ears splayed out. The text from Shane that he had an adoption application should have lifted her spirits, but instead she wanted to cry.

You love that dog just like Shane said. He is the dog of your heart. The dog of your life.

You've been away from him for a few hours, and you miss him so much your heart is going to burst.

She loved Meatball.

She loved Shane.

She loved Wyatt.

Stay, Shane had said. Asked. And she'd said no.

But you can say yes. What you choose to believe is all that matters. Before, that kept you solitary. No husband, no kids, no pets. But now, you can choose to believe that you can *have love.*

That you can *have Shane, Wyatt, Meatball. Furever Paws. The friends you made. You even managed to make nice with Anna Dupree. And you never would have thought that possible in a million years.*

All you have to do is say yes to the love being offered. And risk everything.

She shot up and ran around the side of the inn to her car. She drove to Shane's house, but his truck was gone.

He's at Furever Paws, she knew. *Because you*

couldn't be today. He's there, sitting with Meatball, talking to him nonstop about how he pulled through, how he's going to be okay.

How he got an application.

When she pulled in the gravel lot at Furever Paws, there was Shane's truck, exactly where she expected it to be. She hurried inside to the recuperation room. Shane glanced up from his spot beside Meatball's kennel. The dog's eyes were open but droopy. He was still sedated.

"That man can't adopt Meatball," she said.

Shane nodded. "I know."

She tilted her head. "What do you mean?"

"Phillip can't adopt Meatball because he's spoken for," Shane said. "He's always been spoken for. By you. And me, since I'm hoping you're here to say you're staying."

"I thought I could leave. But I finally realized that I was being my own worst enemy—*choosing* to believe that I can't have what I want most in life, what I've always wanted. Love. A family. You, Shane."

His smile went straight to her heart.

"So I guess that's a yes," he said, stepping closer. "You're staying."

"Oh, Shane. I'm staying. If you'll have me. You and Wyatt."

"And Meatball."

She threw herself into his arms and he hugged her tight. "Thank you for not giving up on me. You could have. But you didn't. I love you so much, Shane. So, so much."

"I love you too," he said, tightening the embrace.

Would she ever stop crying already? She swiped at her eyes.

"I saw your mom today. What she told me helped knock some sense into me. I think we're going to be friends, me and Anna Dupree—and Princess."

"Will wonders ever cease?" he asked. "She and I had a long talk today too. About the past, my father, all that. I think we have a real chance at a new relationship. A much better one."

She rested her head against his chest. "I'm so glad. Thanks to your mom, I'm at peace with the whole is-Elliot-my-father question. I still don't know the actual answer. *He* didn't know." She told him everything his mother had said, his mouth dropping open just as hers had.

"I think that's a really nice ending to a story that always kept you up at night in a bad way, Bethany Robeson. The right ending."

"I'm going to leave the truth under that beautiful maple tree," she said. "Where it belongs. I know what I need to. But your mom also told me that Elliot put photos of my mother and her letters in the box. I'll dig it up for those."

He nodded and wrapped his arms more tightly around her.

"You know what I was thinking about today when I realized that maybe I can stay after all?" she asked.

"What?"

"That the proceeds from Elliot's house—my house—can go to Furever Paws and to a special charitable fund I'd like to start for North Carolina animal rescue centers."

"That's a really great idea," Shane said, holding her close.

"Oh, and you should know—I'm not sure about *five* kids, but I can see a baby brother or sister for Wyatt."

His eyes lit up and he kissed her. "I love you so much, Bethany."

"I love you too. Always have, always will."

She, Shane, Wyatt and Meatball were a family.

And just like her beloved basset hound, Bethany had found her forever home.

Epilogue

A week later, Bethany sat on a chaise in the late March sunshine—it was a gorgeous sixty-five degrees—in Shane's big backyard at their barbecue party, Meatball in his new memory foam bed at her side. The basset hound was on the road to full recovery and was on restricted activity for just a few more days. Then they could resume light walks, but right now, he was being waited on hand and foot by Bethany and Shane.

Princess came ambling over, sniffing Meatball's belly, then actually got right inside the bed and curled up beside him. The two had met earlier in the week when Shane had invited his mother and Princess over to dinner. Princess had given Meatball the stink eye all night, keeping her distance and preferring to be on Anna's lap most of the time. But it appeared she'd changed her tune.

"Aww," Anna said, standing next to Shane at the grill as he placed a cheeseburger on the bun on her plate. "Princess hates all other dogs and most people, but she's warmed up to you three so fast."

"Meatball brings out the best in everyone," Shane said.

Bethany laughed, barely able to believe how much had changed in such a short period of time. She'd officially adopted Meatball. She'd moved into Shane's house. A few nights ago, they'd hosted his ex-wife and her boyfriend and had a great time. Bethany and Anna had gone out to lunch, just the two of them, and the woman had shocked her with a very special gift: the small watercolor painting of Meatball that had been hanging in the lobby of Furever Paws. Anna had gone there to talk about volunteering and when she'd noticed the painting of Meatball, she'd bought it on the spot as a gift. Bethany had thought about buying it herself many times but she hadn't been able to imagine it off the walls of Furever Paws. Now that it was hers, it hung in her office beside her desk in a beautiful frame.

Rebekah, Grant, Lily and Lucas, Josie and Wyatt

were on a huge blanket just a few feet away, Wyatt crawling off and heading straight toward the dog bed on the patio. Princess watched the baby's approach with wide, horrified eyes, then leaped up on Anna's lap the moment the woman sat down beside Bethany.

"Princess, how am I supposed to balance my plate on my lap with you on it? Huh?" Anna asked, giving the Chihuahua a nuzzle. She settled Princess to her side, the dog staring at her burger. "Just a teeny-tiny bite," she said, giving Princess the treat. "Now lie down like a good girl." Princess actually listened, shocking them all.

"You're welcome," Shane called over with a grin.

Anna narrowed her eyes at her son. "You *did* work on training her when I was gone on vacation, didn't you!" she accused, her blue eyes twinkling. "She's so much better behaved. I might even take your Dog Manners 101 class."

"It'll be on the house, too," Shane said.

Birdie and Doc J were standing by the grill, their plates heaped with Josie's incredible potato salad, and the coleslaw and pasta salad that Bethany and Shane had made together. Shane slid a cheeseburger on each of their buns, then made up his own plate and came over, sitting on the other side of Bethany.

The two of them had staggered actual eating time with the Whitakers so that they could all eat in peace without a baby crawling on them and up-ending their plates. Josie was telling the trio a story about a groundhog, not that any of the three were listening. Grant scooped up Wyatt and put him back on the blanket, giving him a floppy bunny to play with. Wyatt touched an ear, his baby friends gig-gling. Rebekah was watching them with a soft smile on her face. She still hadn't made a final decision about whether or not she was coming back to work full time as the assistant director or staying home and volunteering at Furever Paws, but that was just fine with Bethany.

Having Birdie remove the *temporary* from her title would definitely be something of a thrill. Beth-any was no longer temporary at anything. Furever Paws was her job, Meatball was her dog, Shane was her man. And Wyatt would one day be her beloved stepson because she and Shane had already discussed getting married. He said he didn't want to rush into proposing and scare her back to Berryville, but she'd already informed her landlord there that she wouldn't be renewing her lease for her rental condo, and she and Shane would take a drive down to get her stuff.

There wasn't much she wanted to take from her old life, but there was a beautiful framed photograph of her and her mother on the mantel of her living room fireplace, and she'd definitely take that along with the old photo albums that would no longer be painful to look through. With Shane beside her, she had dug up the box under the maple tree at Elliot's house. She'd put the big envelope with the DNA results into a safety deposit box in the bank downtown. But that night, she'd looked at all the pictures of her mother over the decades, her heart full of love, and she'd framed her favorite. It now sat on her bedside table. She'd decided to save the letters for another time, but she had them in the drawer of that table.

After the barbecue, Bethany and Shane would go hang out at Furever Paws, her home away from home, for an hour, visiting the German shepherds who were doing so much better.

Shane leaned over to kiss Bethany on the cheek, then took a bite of his burger. "Not bad at all," he said, taking another bite. He glanced over at his mother. "Um, Mom? I can go make you another one."

"What?" Anna said. "I've barely taken three bites of mine. I can't stop eating the potato salad."

Shane grinned and pointed at Princess, who'd grabbed Anna's burger in her mouth and gone racing off the patio, a piece of the bun going flying.

Everyone laughed, except the babies who'd completely missed the antics of the tiny, furry burger thief.

"You come back here with that, Princess Dupree!" Anna called, running after the Chihuahua, who did *not* do as she was told. Anna finally caught up to her. "You want a bellyache?" She grabbed the burger out of the dog's mouth, letting Princess keep a little wedge of it. "Oh yes, missy. You are definitely taking that manners class."

Shane laughed and took Bethany's hand and kissed it. She looked at him, this man she loved so much, this man who'd changed her life, who'd given her back her dreams. Who'd given her Meatball. Shane had known all along what Bethany hadn't. That home was where the hound was, where Shane was, where baby Wyatt was.

Home was in her heart, now wide open and full of love.

* * * * *

Look for the next book in the
Furever Yours continuity
More Than a Temporary Family
by USA TODAY *bestselling author*
Marie Ferrarella
On sale April 2022,
wherever Harlequin Special Edition books are sold.

#2899 CINDERELLA NEXT DOOR
The Fortunes of Texas: The Wedding Gift
by Nancy Robards Thompson

High school teacher and aspiring artist Ginny Sanders knows she is not Draper Fortune's type. Content to admire her fabulous and flirty new neighbor from a distance, she is stunned when he asks her out. Draper is charmed by the sensitive teacher, but when he learns why she doesn't date, he must decide if he can be the man she needs...

#2900 HEIR TO THE RANCH
Dawson Family Ranch • by Melissa Senate

The more Gavin Dawson shirks his new role, the more irate Lily Gold gets. The very pregnant single mom-to-be is determined to make her new boss see the value in his late father's legacy—her livelihood and her home depend on it! But Gavin's plan to ignore his inheritance and Lily—*and* his growing attraction to her—is proving to be impossible...

#2901 CAPTIVATED BY THE COWGIRL
Match Made in Haven • by Brenda Harlen

Devin Blake is a natural loner, but when rancher Claire Lamontagne makes the first move, he finds himself wondering if he's as content as he thought he was. Is Devin ready to trade his solitary life for a future with the cowgirl tempting him to take a chance on love?

#2902 MORE THAN A TEMPORARY FAMILY
Furever Yours • by Marie Ferrarella

A visit with family was just what Josie Whitaker needed to put her marriage behind her. Horseback-riding lessons were an added bonus. But her instructor, Declan Hoyt, is dealing with his moody teenage niece. The divorced single mom knows just how to help and offers to teach Declan a thing or two about parenting—never expecting a romance to spark with the younger rancher!

#2903 LAST CHANCE ON MOONLIGHT RIDGE
Top Dog Dude Ranch • by Catherine Mann

Their love wasn't in doubt, but fertility issues and money problems have left Hollie and Jacob O'Brien's marriage in shambles. So once the spring wedding season at their Tennessee mountain ranch is over, they'll part ways. Until Jacob is inspired to romance Hollie and her long-buried maternal instincts are revived by four orphaned children visiting the ranch. Will their future together be resurrected, too?

#2904 AN UNEXPECTED COWBOY
Sutton's Place • by Shannon Stacey

Lone-wolf cowboy Irish is no stranger to long, lonely nights. But somehow Mallory Sutton tugs on his heartstrings. The feisty single mom is struggling to balance it all—and challenging Irish's perception of what he has to offer. But will their unexpected connection keep Irish in town...or end in heartbreak for Mallory and her kids?

HSECNM0222

"You still don't belong here." Mariella crossed her arms over her chest, and Alex commanded himself not to notice her body, perfect as it was.

"That makes two of us, and yet here we are."

"I was here first," she muttered. He'd heard the argument before, but it didn't sway him.

"You're not running me off, Mariella. I needed a fresh start, and this is the place I've picked for my home."

"My plan was to leave the past behind me. You are a physical reminder of so many mistakes I've made."

"I can't say that upsets me too much," he lied. It didn't make sense, but he hated that he made her so uncomfortable. Hated even more that sometimes he'd purposely drive by her shop to get a glimpse of her through the picture window. Talk about a glutton for punishment.

She let out a low growl. "You are an infuriating man. Stubborn and callous. I don't even know if you have a heart."

"Funny." He kept his voice steady even as memories flooded him, making his head pound. "That's the rationale Amber gave me for why she cheated with your fiancé. My lack of emotions pushed her into his arms. What was his excuse?"

She looked out at the street for nearly a minute, and Alex wondered if she was even going to answer. He followed her gaze to the park across the street, situated in the center of the town. There were kids at the playground and several families walking dogs on the path that circled the perimeter. Magnolia was the perfect place to raise a family.

If a person had the heart to be that kind of a man—the type who married the woman he loved and set out to be a good husband and father. Alex wasn't cut out for a family, but he liked it in the small coastal town just the same.

"I was too committed to my job," she said suddenly and so quietly he almost missed it.

"Ironic since it was your job that introduced him to Amber."

"Yeah." She made a face. "This is what I'm talking about, Alex. A past I don't want to revisit."

"Then stay away from me, Mariella," he advised. "Because I'm not going anywhere."

"Then maybe I will," she said and walked away.

Don't miss
Wedding Season *by Michelle Major,*
available May 2022 wherever
HQN books and ebooks are sold.

HQNBooks.com

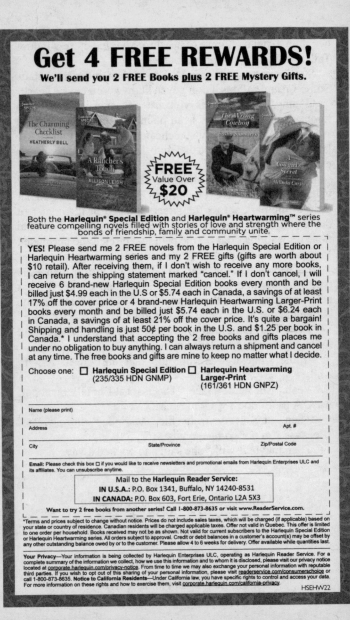